Second Chances

Changes Trilogy ~ Book 2

By Robin Worden

Contents

Chapter 1

Late in the afternoon someone pounded on the front door. I dried my hands on the kitchen towel. I wasn't expecting company. As I passed by the front room, I looked out the bay window. Stephanie's mom's car sat in the drive. As far as I knew, Stephanie had told no one about her condition.

As soon as I turned the knob Stephanie pushed past me, tears streaming from her puffy, red eyes.

"Steph, what's wrong?" I gave the door a shove and followed her into the front room. The sun warmed the plush tan carpet in the window's shape it shone through.

"I almost did it." She sobbed. "I was this close!" She held up her index finger and thumb showing a size of measurement. "But I said I wanted to see it first." She stared at me unblinking.

I hugged her to offer comfort. "What are you talking about?"

She pulled away and grabbed her purse. After rummaging around a few seconds, she slipped a paper into my hand.

I stared at the black and white images trying to decipher what I was looking at.

She stood next to me. "There is the head, the arm." her voice cracked. "I almost killed that, I almost killed my baby!" She covered her mouth with a shaking hand.

I flipped through the ultrasound pictures and smiled at her, relieved by her decision. "But you didn't." I handed them back to her.

She stared at them as she spoke. "I didn't know it looked like a baby. They always made it sound like it was just a blob of flesh." Fresh tears glistened on her cheeks. "But look, see its little foot and toes?"

The sound of screeching tires commanded our attention.

Daniel's work truck and trailer loaded with mowers, skidded to a noisy stop on the street. He darted across the yard with Nick right behind him.

"Oh, no!" Stephanie watched Daniel head toward the front door. "He called me, and I was crying and upset. I told him I was coming to see you."

The front door flew open slamming into the wall, leaving a door handle sized hole in its wake.

He rushed over to Stephanie. "What's wrong? Are you ok? Are you hurt?" He gave her the once over from her head to her feet. He placed his large hands on her shoulders and stared down at her.

The odor of gasoline and mown grass filled the room.

"You were crying and upset, I couldn't understand you at all."

"I'm ok." She rested her hand on his heaving chest. "Well, sort of."

"What?" Confusion filled Daniel's raised voice.

She smiled through the tears. "I wanted to tell you in a better way, but..." She shoved the ultrasound pictures into his waiting hands.

The room was silent as he leafed through the thin pages. "These are," he flipped through them once more with furrowed brows. "these are yours?"

She nodded her head stiffly.

He rubbed his forehead with one hand. "Are you sure?"

Stephanie laughed nervously. "Those are pictures of our baby." Her words hung in the air.

He shifted his weight to his other foot. "What are we going to do?" His eyes never left the pictures.

"I don't know." Her eyes settled on something across the room. "I would abort it and not even tell you, but after seeing it," Her eyes filled with compassion and flickered back to Daniel. "I couldn't."

He remained silent. The atmosphere was becoming uncomfortable. Nick slipped up beside me, grabbed my hand, and led me out of the room.

We sat on the couch in the den allowing Daniel and Stephanie some alone time.

"What do you think they will do?" I whispered.

He shook his head and stared at the fireplace. "I don't know. A baby is a lifelong deal. I'm so glad that's not us." He squeezed my hand.

No chance of that happening, I thought to myself. In order for that kind of thing to happen you have to do something, and so far, I had been unsuccessful in my attempts.

The quietness was deafening.

Nick's phone rang. "Yeah?"

I recognized Daniel's voice on the other end.

"On my way."

He stood and shoved his phone into his pocket. "I've got to go."

I stood and eyed him.

He shrugged. "I don't know." His eyes darted toward the front room and then back. He hugged me goodbye.

I followed him into the entryway.

He examined the hole in the wall. "I'll fix that later." He closed the door.

Stephanie stood in the front room staring out the window. The situation had sucked the oxygen out of the room. After the guys drove off, she continued to stare out the window. As much as I wanted to know what Daniel said, I wanted more for my friend to have her time and talk when she was ready. We stood silent for several minutes as she clutched the pictures to her chest.

She turned and stared at me with puffy eyes. "He said he needed time to think." She looked exhausted. "I told him I loved him, and he could have all the time he needed." A fat teardrop ran down her cheek. "I'm going home and tell Mom what's going on." She lugged her purse onto her shoulder. "I'm keeping it. If Daniel wants to be part of the baby's life that's great, and if he wants nothing to do with us..." Her lips trembled. "Then that's fine too." Determination replaced her tired appearance.

I put my arm around her shoulders as we walked to the door. "Do you want me to go with you?"

She let out a long breath. "No, I need to do this on my own. I'll call you later."

I closed the door, wishing her luck.

Daniel's reaction wasn't what I thought it might be, but that didn't make him a bad guy.

The rest of the afternoon my mind was on Stephanie. I was glad she didn't abort the baby. This was our senior year. I could only imagine the torment a pregnant girl would face in high school. I was sure she could handle it, but if Daniel wasn't backing her, it would be a lot more difficult.

She called, and we talked for a long time. She decided not to attend public school, which started in a few weeks. Instead, she would attend an alternative school for pregnant teens that was close. Her Mom was disappointed and upset with her. After an hour of ranting and raving, she calmed down and told Stephanie if she wanted to keep the baby, they would figure something out. Stephanie had no plans on telling her Dad until it became a necessity. I heard the hurt in her voice when she told me she still had not heard from Daniel. I had not heard from Nick either. We changed the subject.

My senior year hadn't even started, and it was turning out to be different from what I had envisioned. The changes I wanted to make in my life did not involve going through my senior year without my best friend. I said goodbye to Steph and sent a text message to Nick.

He text back he was with Daniel and we would talk later.

I only had two weeks before Nick left for college. He was so busy recently that I rarely got to see him. Maybe that was a good thing. I missed him already, and he hadn't even gone anywhere.

Chapter 2

It was Sunday afternoon, and Nick was packed and ready to go to college. The day I had dreaded for so long had arrived, there was no way around it. His plans for the day included going to church and having lunch with his family before leaving. I declined going along, afraid my emotions could get the best of me. I didn't want to interrupt their family time together, at least that is what I kept telling myself to keep from calling him to come get me. He promised he would see me before he left.

The hands on the clock barely moved, tormenting me in two ways; too slow to get to see him and too fast because I would be unable to see him for at least a week.

I cleaned the house from top to bottom and searched for something else to take up time. I gave up on reading when I couldn't keep my mind on the storyline. I didn't want to say goodbye. Anxiety seeped from every pore of my body. I couldn't wrap my mind around how much I wanted to be with Nick all the time; how I needed to be near him. He was my addiction, and this addict was going to have major withdrawals.

I watched him pull into the driveway. I made myself wait for him at the door. We sat in the den and talked. I skipped around the subject of him leaving. I knew this day would come, and I still was not prepared. I had avoided that line of thought like the plague, knowing it would only bring suffering and torment. He would only be a few hours away and he promised to come home on weekends. Part of my heart was being ripped out and taken with him.

The hands of time sped up, and it was time for him to leave though it felt like he had just arrived. We stood in the den in an embrace I didn't want to end. I rested my cheek against his chest listening to the rhythm of his heart, feeling his muscles beneath his shirt, and breathing him in.

"Are you going to be okay?" He whispered against my hair.

I nodded my head and clung to him.

He chuckled. "You're a terrible liar, even when you don't say a word."

If I didn't let go of him, he couldn't leave. A childish thought I knew, and one that left me with little hope of working.

He gently pushed against my shoulders.

I pulled more him closer.

"Hey now." He rubbed my back. "Come on." He pushed against my shoulders again.

I loosened my death grip enough to allow a ruler's length between us. I stared at his shirt where there was evidence that my eyes had betrayed my valiant quest to be strong.

"Look at me."

I shifted my vision upward as a lone tear broke free.

He raised his eyebrows as he wiped it away with his thumb. "I thought we agreed, no tears?" His voice was soft with compassion.

I felt like a scolded child. I pursed my lips together for fear that if I spoke, more emotion would come tumbling out. I stared into his blue eyes that engulfed me. I would miss those. My eyes slid down to his lips. I would miss those too. I took in a deep breath and just as I thought the dam that held that emotion back would break; he lowered those perfect lips to mine.

I lost all thought except for the incredible feeling that burned deep within my heart.

I stood in the driveway and watched his car disappear around the corner. I shook my head at the hold this boy had on me and it was a hold I didn't want to be free from.

I still needed to get my own things in order for school tomorrow. I trudged off to my room. With Steph and the guys gone I had to figure out a way of getting to and from school. I wanted change, but not all of this.

Mom brought take out from a restaurant, so we didn't have to cook. She worked nights, so at least she could give me a ride to and from school. I could survive the stigma of being dropped off by a parent. Mom gave me space; she wasn't overprotective or overbearing. Before Nick came along I was okay to be alone, but he had changed that within a few months. Mom and I made small talk during dinner.

I finished eating and headed back to my room to complete what I had started. I turned on the radio to drown out the silence. The song that flooded my room was the same one that Stephanie, Daniel, Nick and I had done our dance routine to at the prom. I went through some moves and smiled. Dancing wasn't so bad after all; in fact, I liked it. A change that had occurred that was a positive one.

I picked up my phone several times to text Nick only to put it back down on my bed. He told me he would let me know once he got there and unpacked. Knowing he was a few hours away and I couldn't just see him when I wanted, hung on the edge of my thoughts all night. A fear was hiding within that had not made itself completely known yet. It lurked in the shadows of my mind, just out of reach of rationale. Nick, my defender, was no longer around to save the day.

I looked over my class schedule mapping out in my mind where each class was. This year's load of classes would be the hardest yet. I had hopes of going to college and needed to keep a good grade point average. I didn't want to be as uptight this year, but with this schedule, I would be hard-pressed to have time during the week to do something other than homework. Andrea's words bounced around in my thoughts of her going to the same college as Nick. If his ex-girlfriend was going to be there, then I would be there too.

Chapter 3

The alarm rang letting me know it was time to rise and shine. I wasn't too sure about the shining part, and the rising was having trouble too. I shut my alarm off and went about my daily, school morning routine. Funny how I had not followed that routine all summer, yet somehow magically, I slipped right back into it with ease.

I stood in front of the school ready to take on my senior year. A slight breeze kept the morning from being too unbearable. Things were different, and that was ok. I wanted to break out of my old self, have a new start. I walked through the doors with my head held high. Being a senior had perks, I needed to figure out what they were. I lived in this town forever and went to school with these kids my whole life, give or take a few that had moved in or away.

The first day of school was going well. It was different not having Nick and Daniel around at lunch, never a dull moment when those two were together and it involved food. I sat alone at our old lunch table reliving memories.

Jasper was in a few of my classes this year. He was still carrying his Bible around and people were still talking about it and making fun of him behind his back. Some things never change. I was thankful for his prayers during Nick's stay in the hospital after the attack in the park, when Nick nearly lost his life.

I had Andrea in two classes. She stared at me smugly, while commenting to some of her friends about Nick being at college, and how she was going to the same college next year. Instead of voicing the comments that formed on the tip of my tongue, I ignored her and stared out the window. The sun was shining; it looked like a perfect day. Andrea was giggling a little too loud, and I was sure it was for my benefit. My thoughts drifted to Nick and how his first day on the big campus was going. He had sent me a text late last night letting me know he made it and he would get with me later. I had two periods left and now that my brain was in Nick mode, it would feel like two years.

The first week of separation went by easier than I expected. It was already Friday night and Nick was coming home. It seemed like such a long time since I had seen him. We had been dating for a while, but my heart still raced at the thought of him.

I finished my chores and got the dreaded homework out of the way. I sat staring out the window waiting. He was stopping off at his parent's house and saying hi, and then he would head over here. Anticipation was building; I was dancing on the edge of excitement. Every movement on the road caught my immediate attention.

As soon as I saw his car, I was out the door in a flash, no prompting needed. He was barely out of his car before I securely wrapped my arms around him. I buried my face in his chest. I closed my eyes taking it in, hoping I would never have to let go again.

Somewhere deep inside familiarity sprang up from my past. When I was younger, I would run out to meet my Dad, much in the same way, when he would come home from long business trips. I guess Mom and I were not as important to him as he was to us, or he wouldn't have left. I pushed those thoughts out of my mind; I refused to allow anything to interfere with this moment.

He laughed. "Hi!"

I stared up at his cute lopsided smile and melted like chocolate in a small child's hand amid a hot summer day. "I missed you so much!" I blurted out.

That brought another laugh from him. "I missed you too." He stroked my cheek as he gazed down at me. His eyes held me captive. I knew what was coming and excitement shot through my body from my toes to the top of my head. His lips were soft and though it was short, it was the sweetest yet. My heart pounding in my ears drowned out the songbirds. Not ready for reality yet, I sighed as he pulled away.

We sat and talked most of the night. A last-minute change in accommodations kept him from being roommates with Daniel. Instead, his roommate was a guy named Jeb. The more Nick talked, the more the excitement was clear. Jeb was a believer and went to church. There was a Christian outreach on campus they were getting involved in. It was nice to see Nick smile so much. I was glad things were going well for him. My selfish side wished he hated it and would come back home.

He didn't have classes with Daniel, and they were not roommates. They were a few floors apart in the dorm and had run into one another more than once. Daniel had stayed on campus this weekend instead of coming home. I didn't push for any information about Daniel and Stephanie.

The time for Nick to leave came too soon. Even though I would see him the next day, I didn't want him to leave. My heart yearned to be with him twenty-four seven. I reluctantly said goodbye.

The next couple of weekends were the same, Nick would come home, we would spend time together, and then he was off to college again. Two weekends in a row he didn't come home at all. He had gotten involved in the church thing on campus and they had planned events on those weekends. I was sure there were more to come, I should just get used to it. I asked myself more than once how I could be jealous of a church. Each time the answer was the same, it took Nick away from me.

Those were bad weekends for me. I spent time with Stephanie, whose waist was rapidly expanding. She liked the alternative school for pregnant teens. She and Daniel had hashed things out. He wanted to quit college and work for his Dad full time, just as Stephanie predicted. That was why he had stayed at school instead of coming home, he was trying to get it lined up to come back home and somehow save his scholarship at the same time. She convinced him to stay in college and assured him she was fine. Daniel said there was never a doubt of whether he would stay and stick it out with her; he was just trying to figure out which was the correct next step for him and his new family. He was all in, stating he loved Stephanie and the baby more than anything else. I was happy for Steph while feeling miserable for myself.

Nick and I talked and sent texts to each other; it was just hard for me not seeing him. I hated this long-distance relationship ordeal. We were no closer to being intimate with one another than before which was something I was really pushing to change. Andrea making her little comments about things between her and Nick only added fuel to the desire to know him in the same way she did. I tried to play it off like I knew what she was talking about. I seriously had no clue, and it ate at me like a cancer. She was an itch under my skin I could not reach no matter how hard I tried. She must have known because she only dug in that much deeper.

The weekdays drug by, and the weekends blew by like a whirlwind, leaving me lonely.

Nick was more involved than ever in the church thing and would quote scriptures in the texts he sent. When we would talk on the phone, it seemed all he wanted to talk about was God and the Bible. Every time I would shift our conversation toward us, he would figure out a way to bring God into it.

The void was rumbling more and more lately. The fear that was hiding was making itself known. I thought I was the most important thing to him, but I was being replaced.

Chapter 4

As I watched Nick drive off, I wrapped my arms around my waist trying to keep warmth in my sweatshirt. The wind whipped around me blasting me with frigid air. It was already November, and I was ready for some extra time with Nick during the holidays. Maybe being around me, instead of that cult church group, would bring the old Nick back. I had failed again getting any further with him than just a few kisses. Those kisses left me wondering how much better other things would be with him. I determined I would find out and some extra time alone with him may be all I needed. Andrea's continual comments were digging into my brain like poisoned needles.

With Nick being gone, I had plowed into my schoolwork and got all A's. If I could keep it up, I would be exempt from finals, which would mean a few more days off to let my brain cells regroup for next semester.

Monday and Tuesday went by quickly. The weather had turned even colder making me wonder if some severe weather would come along and keep Nick from me, besides the church on campus. Maybe things would play out in my favor and he would get stranded here at home. The thought of us snuggling up by the fire brought a smile to my lips. A picture of Nick dressed only in his red jogging shorts popped into my head. I mentally scanned each muscle on his body that burned itself into my brain.

After dinner, I got out my math and sprawled across my bed going over formulas, for lack of anything more interesting to do. Nick told me he would be out of pocket for the evening doing something with Jeb for the campus outreach.

"Emma."

"Emma!"

My body didn't want to wake up. I struggled to open one eye halfway and squinted up at Mom.

"I'm getting ready to leave for work."

I nodded my head at her and dropped it back down to the pillow. Mom was working graveyard so that meant it was bedtime. I wanted to go back to sleep, but thinking of all that bacteria multiplying in my mouth overnight got me awake enough to stumble into the bathroom and get ready for bed.

I put my book in my bag and turned out the light before climbing under the covers. Parts of the sheets were warm where I had sprawled out moments before. I snuggled under the covers listening to the wind howl outside.

The wind used to scare me when I was little. Dad would come in and be the brave knight. He would go to the window pretending to fight with the wind. With victory accomplished he would tell me, "I've defeated the wind, Princess! It can only make a noise now. No harm will come to you, my lady." He would bow and kiss the top of my hand. I felt like royalty and he was my hero coming to my rescue. That was before him and Mom's problems started. After the problems began I had to fend for myself, being told I needed to be strong. I forced the memory out of my mind, biting back feelings of resentment.

The garage door whined and squeaked to get into the open position. Mom was on her way to work. I watched the headlights from her car flicker across my windows as she backed out of the garage and then start down the street. The howling wind was interrupted once more by the prehistoric garage door motor powering the door back down. We almost bought a new fancy opener last year that had the sensors on it. It would kick the door back up if a small child or animal got in the way. Since we didn't have a small child or animal, we kept the one we had. It still worked it was just super loud. Once this one kicked the bucket we would ante up for a new quieter one.

As I drifted off to sleep, my subconscious registered a noise. It must be the wind I assured myself groggily and snuggled deeper into the blankets pulling them up around my ears. A few minutes had passed, and I heard something else. My brain replayed the noise over and over in my head. It didn't sound like a noise the wind could make; it sounded like someone was in the house.

I rolled over and looked at the glowing numbers on my clock. I bet Mom forgot something again. I threw the blankets back and headed down the hallway toward the kitchen already planning jokes about her being old and forgetful.

As I walked, I realized there weren't any lights on. Maybe she got what she needed and left again.

"Mom?" I felt my way along the wall wishing I had flipped a light switch on.

No answer.

I slowed my approach and listened. Thanks to a little adrenaline my body had kicked into my bloodstream, I was more awake now. The wind was still blowing outside with gusts now and then that sounded like they could probably rip screens off. I sighed as I remembered the loose screen on the kitchen window. I relaxed feeling silly for getting so worked up over nothing. I walked to the fridge and pulled out some orange juice. I left the door open for light and grabbed a cup. After a few gulps, I rinsed the cup and left it in the sink. I heard the rattling of the screen as I closed the refrigerator door.

Maybe I would text Nick and see if he was still awake, maybe he was studying. I walked out of the kitchen and headed to my bedroom.

A wave of uneasiness swept over me. I peered into the darkened den, nothing unusual attracted my attention. I turned the opposite direction and stared into the darkness at the front door. Everything was in place. I scanned further to the left. My breath caught in my throat. My heartbeat tripled at the sight of the silhouette of a person standing across the room. My mind raced through a hundred different plans of action at once.

"Hi, Emma."

The male voice sounded familiar.

My muddled mind tried to figure out the plan of action needed, who the outline of this person was, and why they were in my living room in the middle of the night. My brain confirmed none of this added up to anything good. I stared at the figure unable to move, or even speak. My brain was screaming warnings and commands, my body just wasn't listening.

The laugh that came from the room caused the hair on the back of my neck to stand on end. I knew it was a sign of danger that my body was sending me. I stood frozen with terror. It couldn't be! It wasn't possible! The figure moved towards me. I assessed the height and build, and it was a perfect match. I shook my head in disbelief.

"You should lock the door that leads to the garage. Somebody might sneak in one day." A hint of humor wrapped around his words.

Panic mixed with fear and shot through my body like a torpedo. I sprinted toward my bedroom. He tackled me from behind, crashing me into the wall before we both hit the floor. I fought and pushed until I could get turned around to face him so he didn't have as much of an advantage... yet.

I needed to get to my cell phone.

I lashed out with my fists striking whatever part of his body I could. It did not seem to affect him, I might as well have been pounding on a wall. My vision blurred with tears from my nose smacking into the wall.

Knowing he could overpower me, I continued to kick and squirm. I was halfway there. If I could just get to my room, I could shut the door and lock it. I wiggled around until I worked my knee into his abdomen. It felt like a rock. I pushed until I created a small amount of space that separated his body from mine. I struggled to keep my arms free. If he pinned me down, it would all be over. I got my right foot in between us and pushed. I worked to get my other foot in between us. With a grunt, I kicked both feet straight out as hard as I could.

He tumbled backward into the darkness.

I scrambled through my doorway and slammed the door. To my horror, he had got his foot wedged between the door and the frame, keeping it from closing completely.

He laughed in the hallway as I tried in vain to get the door shut. He was toying with me as if I had a chance against him. Why was he even allowing this facade to continue?

"Aren't you going to invite me in, baby?" His voice boomed with sarcasm.

I looked over my shoulder to judge the distance between me and the nightstand where my phone was charging. I kept my foot lodged against the bottom of the door and stretched for the nightstand. It was too far away. I had to figure out a way to get to my phone and dial 9-1-1 before he could get me. He was pushing the door open; it groaned against the struggle that was pushing from both sides. My time for ideas was up.

I dove for my nightstand, sending my lamp crashing to the floor. I grabbed my phone, bounced across the bed, and landed with a thud on the floor. I got 9-1- typed in before he ripped it from my fingers.

He crouched in front of me and smashed the phone against the wall next to my head. He tossed the pieces over his shoulder.

I scooted backward into the corner. I sat on the floor trembling on the inside. My mind kept flashing back to the park which only caused more fear.

"What do you want?" My voice trembled as much as my insides.

"You know what I want." He sneered.

"My purse is over there." I pointed a shaking finger toward the door.

The evil in his quiet laughter made me cringe. My eyes darted from him to the doorway. He was too close. If I ran for the door, I would have to climb back over the bed, it would slow me down; I would never make it.

"Stand up." his tone was cold.

I watched him with wide eyes, not knowing if I should obey

or stay where I was. My brain sifted through different books and movies with similar scenarios; maybe something would work. Should I defy his demands or should I do what he said? Flashes of him in action at the park flew through my mind, the blood, the pain, the sweat…

"Stand up!" his voice echoed off the walls.

I slowly rose to my feet using the two walls for support.

He reached toward the window and opened the blinds flooding the room with the dim light from outside.

The light confirmed his identity and fear raced through my body producing a visible shutter.

"Are you scared?" he taunted.

I nodded, trying to sink into the walls.

"You should be." He reached into his pocket and produced a small piece of plastic. "Thanks for letting me borrow your driver's license. It made it a lot easier to find you." He held it out.

I stared at it, motionless.

He shrugged and carelessly tossed it into the air behind him.

He drew his words out. "I've watched your house. I know when you come, and I know when you go. I know your routine." He chuckled. "I even know your Mom's routine." He peeled off his jacket revealing his chiseled body and threw it in the door's direction. His eyes raked over my body.

I wished now I had worn my long sleeve, long pant pajamas instead of the black tank and shorts I had chosen.

"I was hoping for the red ones." His eyes settled on my face.

I stared at him. How did he know I had a set like this one that was red? Had he been going through my drawers; but how? One of them stole my wallet, not my keys.

He seemed amused by my reaction. "Oh, I've been here many nights." He wore a smug expression. "I've watched you sleeping."

Fear took more of a hold, knowing he had been here in the house when I was here sleeping made me nauseous.

He cocked his head and raised his eyebrows. "You talk in your sleep."

Dread filtered in drowning out the fear. I could scarcely breathe. What information he held, I did not want to know.

"Seems you are having trouble getting little Nicky to give you what you really want."

As soon as the thought flashed through my mind, I snapped into action and slapped him hard across the face.

He drew the back of his hand across his mouth and laughed at the dark smear. "I think you'll find me a little more willing than him, to give you what you want."

The arrogance in his voice made me ill. My hand was already halfway to his face again.

He thrust his arm forward wrapping his fingers around my neck and slammed my head back against the unforgiving wall. He moved forward until he was inches away from my face.

"Say my name." His breath was hot on my face and reeked of cigarettes and alcohol. "Say it!" He squeezed until I thought I might lose consciousness.

As hard as I tried, I could not pry loose even one finger of his steely grip. The edges of my vision were darkening, little white dots danced before my eyes. "Des."

My voice was barely audible.

Pinning my body to the wall with his, he mashed his lips against mine. The taste of blood brought back unwanted memories, feelings of fear, desperation, mourning, and loss.

"No!" I screamed in his face.

He mocked me with his laughter.

I tore one hand free and raked my nails across his skin.

He backed off holding the side of his face.

I sprang onto the bed, headed for the door. Something tangled around my feet, slamming me forward. I prepared for the impact of the floor; instead, it was the mattress. I only made it a few feet.

He was close, too close.

I lunged forward, my eyes locked on the doorway.

He grabbed a handful of my hair and jerked my head up, forcing the rest of my body to follow.

"No!" I gasped. "No! No! No!" I kept repeating those words over and over as if it would finally sink in and he would stop and leave me alone.

The back of his hand caught me across the jaw, jerking my head to the side. I tried to fight back; the crushing blows from his fists were just too much. I fought and struggled against him for what felt like hours. My arms and legs were too heavy for me to lift. The fight inside me was gone, no more adrenaline was available. My eyes swelled, and the taste of blood made me gag. I wanted it to end, to be over. Hot tears drenched my face when I realized I couldn't outlast him, and there was no one to save me this time; it was hopeless.

The sound of fabric ripping filled my ears.

I turned my head and closed my eyes forcing myself to a better place, a safer place in my mind, where he couldn't follow.

I willingly lost track of time.

Chapter 5

He grabbed a hand full of my hair and jerked. "If anybody finds out about this, I'll be back; and I won't be so nice." With that comment, he moved away.

I was too afraid, too tired, to move. Was he really gone or was he waiting for me to move before he attacked again? I was as still as possible, barely breathing, listening for any hint he might still be in the house. I slowly moved and scanned my room. No sign of him in here. I closed my door and locked it. I sunk to the floor in a heap. Tears came with realization of the horror that just occurred.

When the sobs subsided, exhaustion and shock ruled my body. I hugged my knees close to my chest, hoping that by doing so, it would hold me together. The smell of stale cigarette smoke clung to my skin. I suddenly felt filthy. I could still smell him. I could feel his hands, it was sickening. I grabbed my robe holding it out away from me; I didn't want it near me until I was clean.

The sky outside was a light grey, Mom would be home soon. Mom.

How would I explain this, how would I... shame overpowered me. Hot tears flooded my swollen cheeks. I couldn't tell anybody about this terrible, terrible thing.

I opened my door just a crack. I eyed the darkened hallway; it was lighter toward the den and the living room. I listened closely. After a few moments, I opened the door. I kept my eyes on the end of the hall looking for any signs of movement. I darted across the hallway into the bathroom, locking the door behind me. I turned the water on as hot as I could stand it.

I lathered and scrubbed and washed and then did it again and again. I had to be sure I got every inch of him off me. If I scrubbed any harder, my skin would bleed. More tears disappeared down the drain.

I wrapped my robe snugly around my body. I cracked the door and peeked down the hallway. I listened again. He must have left by now. If he knew our routines, he would know Mom would be home soon. I flew across the hall and slammed my door, locking it behind me. I moved my bookshelf up against the door. It wouldn't keep someone out if they were intent on coming in, but it would sure make a noise. I could climb out the window if I needed to.

I studied my reflection in my full-length mirror. There was no way I could go to school or anywhere else for a few days. I gawked at the bruises and swollen features of my face, no way to cover that with makeup. I could hide the marks around my neck where his fingers had almost squeezed the life from my body, by wearing a turtleneck. Long sleeves would cover the bruises on my wrists from his strong hands. I could hide the other parts of my body with clothing. No one else would see those parts of my body. I certainly did not have to worry about Nick seeing them.

Nick.

Sadness overwhelmed me. If I could just hear his voice; if I could just call him for a minute. I clutched my robe around me and searched the floor for my phone. I found part of it lying at the end of the bed, the other part was against the wall on the other side of the room. Would I be able to hide it from him, would he know? Would he still love me? Fresh tears stung my eyes.

My body was feeling the effects from the wrestling match. Every muscle screamed at me as I pulled my clothes on. I tried to push the other part out of my head and pull myself together mentally.

I stood staring into space; not wanting to believe this happened. I was so tired, but I didn't want to sleep; I was afraid to close my eyes. I turned toward the bed. It wasn't fair! It wasn't right! This shouldn't have happened! I tore the blankets and sheets off the bed. I ripped the sheets with my bare hands. Rage grew inside me. I flung the bedding into my closet along with my torn clothing and slammed the door. I pulled and tugged on the mattress. I fought with it until it was off the box springs. I fell onto it pounding it with my fists. Tears streaked down my swollen, hot cheeks. My emotions were a roller coaster; I wanted to get off, but there was no stopping it.

The grating sound of the garage door opening made my pulse race. Was it possible he was still in the house? No, he said he had been here several nights and knew our routines. If he wanted to hurt Mom, he would have done it already. It was me he was after, and he had gotten what he wanted.

I kept still, holding my breath. The knock on my door sent my scurrying across the floor in fear.

"Emma, are you awake?"

My heart pounded so loud in my ears I could barely hear her through the door. "Yeah, I'm awake." My voice sounded anxious. I tried to relax against the wall, mentally willing my heart to slow.

"You better hurry if you want me to take you to school."

I couldn't step outside my room, let alone go out into public.

"Did you hear me?"

My mind struggled to find an excuse, with all that happened and no sleep, it wasn't functioning on all levels. "I'm not going!" I blurted out.

"Why not?" She demanded.

My head was swimming.

She rattled the door handle. "What's going on?" More rattling. "Why is the door locked?"

"Don't come in!" I scrambled to my mattress trying to get it back in place, so I could hide under the blankets. There wasn't anything to hide under. My room was a mess; she couldn't come in. Panic was setting in fast. My brain was going in circles. I closed my eyes wishing everything and everyone would just disappear. My eyes popped open with the idea that bounced into my head. "I'm sick."

"What?"

I faked a cough. "I'm sick. You can't come in or you might get it. I've been up all night."

A pause in the rattling.

I knew I was a terrible liar. The last part was true; I had been up all night. I waited with bated breath.

"Oh. Are you okay? Can I get you anything?" Her tone shifted from suspicion to concern.

If she only knew the truth, but I was too ashamed.

"No, I don't' want anything." That wasn't true, I wanted to go back and erase last night.

"If you need anything, call me or text me ok?"

I looked at my phone in pieces on the floor. "Sure," I breathed.

That sufficed her for now. I did not know how long I could play the sick card before she demanded I go to the doctor. I hoped it was long enough for the bruises and swelling to disappear.

It was daylight and Mom was home, so I felt safe enough to let my guard down. I drifted off to sleep for a few minutes. I was already dreading nightfall when Mom would leave to go to work. Would he come back again? If he got away with one night would he push his luck with more? A light rap on the door interrupted my thoughts.

"Are you awake?" Mom's voice was low.

"Huh?" I tried to sound sick and half asleep.

"I'm sorry if I woke you honey, but I made you some chicken noodle soup and there's a bottle of water. Can you open the door?"

I glanced at the clock; it would get dark soon. "Can you leave them on the tray outside the door and when I feel better I'll get them?"

"Sure. Is there anything else I can do?" I pictured her standing outside the door with a motherly look of concern.

"Tonight, when you leave," My voice broke.

"What honey? I can't hear you." I heard her twist the knob.

I cleared my throat and tried again. "When you leave tonight, can you make sure you wait until the garage door closes all the way before you take off, and can you lock the door going out to the garage?"

There was silence.

"Please?"

"Uh, okay. Why?"

I had to think fast; it had to be something believable, but not outrageous. "I think an animal, or something got into the garage last night when you left." My throat tightened as I recalled that animal.

She laughed lightly. "Okay. I'll watch and make sure nothing crawls under the door before I leave."

"Thanks, Mom." I settled back into my corner with a blanket from my closet. I had shoved the blankets and sheets from my bed in the back of my closet to get them as far away from me as possible. Once my face was back to normal, I would burn them. I would come up with a story if their disappearance became known.

As soon as I heard the garage door, I snagged the food from the hallway and shut my door, making sure I locked it. I lugged the bookshelf the front of the door to stand as a sentinel. If Mom thought I wasn't eating, it would cause a quicker trip to the doctor. I dumped it into my trash can; I had no appetite.

I could not blame noises on the wind tonight. It found a better place to hang out, leaving the house eerily still. The house creaked and groaned more than I ever remembered.

Nervous sweat drenched my clothes. Half the night I kept my eyes glued to the door, the other half I glued them to my windows. The night lasted an eternity. I sighed with relief as daylight broke; it was Friday morning.

I struggled to get the bookcase out of the way and hurried into the bathroom scrubbing every inch of my body. The bruises weren't going away as quick as I had hoped. Friday meant that Nick would come home. I prepared to pull the sick card all weekend, but I wasn't sure I could get by with it.

The garage door opening broke the silence, causing me to flinch. Mom was home early. I grabbed my things in my arms and darted across the hall to my room. I stuck the tray with the empty containers back out into the hallway for Mom to find.

A few minutes later the knock on my door was not quiet, like last time. "Emma?" Her voice was loud.

Fear shot through me. Did she know; could she have found out somehow?

"Yeah?"

She wiggled the knob finding it locked fast. "Are you ok? You didn't answer your phone."

"I'm a little better. I think my phone is broke. I tripped and it kind of broke into pieces." Again, half lie and half-truth. I held my breath.

"Are you ok?"

"Yeah, but the phone isn't."

"Do you want me to fix you some breakfast or something?" She rattled the dishes on the tray.

"No not yet, but maybe later."

"Nick called and said he couldn't get a hold of you last night or this morning. Your phone being broken would explain it."

"He's..." I cleared my throat to remove the fear that resonated through my voice. "He's not coming over tonight, is he?"

"He said he was."

My heart moved into my throat.

She continued. "I told him you were sick, but he said he wasn't afraid. He said he is praying for you." She laughed. "He's a sweet boy. Maybe some company will help you feel better."

I was too tired from being up all night. I didn't want to think about an escape plan right now. I went back to my corner and curled up in my robe and blanket.

I fought to keep the memories of Wednesday night out of my head. I shuddered at the thought of his hands on me. I rubbed my arms and legs briskly to get that feeling to subside. I closed my eyes hoping for peaceful rest.

I dreamed Des came back and I couldn't get away. I was running down a long corridor full of locked doors. No matter how hard I tried, I couldn't get away.

I awoke to someone beating on my door. My heart thumped violently in my chest. I tried to get the sleep cobwebs cleared out of my brain. I wasn't in the corridor. I was in my room, and it was dark.

"Emma, are you ok? Open the door!" Mom's voice was loud and demanding.

"I'm okay." Emotion rang out in my voice. "It was just a bad dream."

"Em?"

My eyes shot to the door. Was he already here? I squinted at the clock; it was six o'clock. I closed my eyes for a moment. I hadn't concocted a story or excuse, not that he would believe it, anyway.

Mom was telling Nick to just break the door down. The door-knob was rattling. He was trying to unlock it with something.

"I'm okay!" I shouted. I stood, not knowing what to do to keep them out.

"Then open the door." They responded in unison.

"I can't." I whispered. The trembling that had started on the inside, made its way to my limbs.

More knocking.

"Just leave me alone." I cried.

"What's wrong, Em? I'm opening the door, so stay back."

"No! Don't come in!" I was desperate. "Please, Nick! Please, don't come in!"

The loud crack and thud made me cry out with fear. Fear of what they would see, fear of what they would now learn, and fear of what they would think about me. The door flung open into the wall behind it. Light from the hallway spilled in.

"Em?"

"Emma?"

I watched their forms step into the room. Their heads turned left to right, scanning for me. The overhead light made me squint. I watched in slow motion as they took in the destruction in front of them; the overturned lamp, the bed, the phone on the floor in pieces and then... me. The confusion written on their faces and in their eyes was replaced horror as they took in my appearance.

"Are you ok?" Mom took a step closer. "What happened?" Her eyes swept back and forth over the room as though if she looked hard enough, it was written somewhere for her to read. "Did you get into a fight at school?" Her eyes settled on me. I could see her trying to work it out in her head. "Were you attacked?"

The lights were coming on and the look on her face told me the connection she was making distressed her.

"Was that why you wanted me to make sure the garage door was down before I left?" She covered her mouth.

I put up a hand to halt her advancement toward me.

"Oh, God." She whispered. "It happened Wednesday night, didn't it?" She looked horrified. "Why didn't you tell me?"

I shook my head at her, trying to hold it all together.

"I'm calling the police." She sprinted out of the room.

Nick, who had remained motionless, now depleted half the space between us with a few long strides. I held out a shaky hand as a warning to keep his distance. The bruising on my wrist was visible now. I was sure the ones on my neck were too.

The pain etched on his face took my breath away.

He fought to hold his composure. "Do you know who it was?"

"It was a guy from the park." Tears filled my eyes. "It was Des."

"What?" He looked shocked. "But how..."

"He stole my license." My lips trembled.

His eyes darted to the bare bed for a moment before settling back on me. I knew the question he wanted to ask, but couldn't bring himself to do it.

Waves of shame crashed down on me. The dam of control was cracking. I nodded my head ever so slightly.

He hunched forward resting his hands just above his slightly bent knees. He looked like someone had just knocked the breath out of him and he was trying to get it back. When he rose, his face reflected anguish.

He lunged forward and wrapped his arms around me. "Oh, Em." His voice echoed pain.

My body exploded into panic mode. I pushed him, hitting him and screaming at the top of my lungs. "Get away, get away from me!" All I could see was Des's face and feel his hands. I retreated to my corner. "Don't touch me." My puffy cheeks were wet with tears. "Please, please don't touch me." I begged quietly. My body trembled with fear I could not stop. When I opened my eyes, Nick stood with a tortured look on his face.

He shook his head, "What did he do to you?" A tear trailed down his face. The sorrow and pain soon gave way to anger. He clenched his fists at his sides. "I'll find him, and when I do, he will pay for this!"

Mom rushed into the room, phone pressed close to her ear. Her hollow voice recited our address.

Nick pounded his finger against his phone and placed it up to his ear. "Come get me at Emma's."
He waited for the person on the other end to respond. "Yes, now! I'll explain once you get here." He tossed the phone on my bed. "I'll call you later." The cloud of rage parted for a moment, revealing extreme torment. "I love you, Em."

"I'm sorry, Nick, I don't know what happened, I..." I crumpled to the floor unable to stand any longer.

He shook his head. "You don't have to be sorry for anything; I'll take care of it." He headed for the door and then turned back, his jaw tightly clenched. "I promise he will pay for what he's done!"

The police officers arrived at the house as Nick was leaving. The female officer questioned me while the male officer took my bedding and clothing and put them into bags marked as evidence.

They wanted to call an ambulance to take me to the hospital. I talked them into letting Mom drive me instead. All I needed was to draw more attention to the situation and an ambulance arriving would likely turn more heads.

The female officer tried to make it easier for me, but she had to ask questions, questions that made me uncomfortable. This was a part of my life I didn't want known by anyone even if they were complete strangers.

Neighbors looked out their windows. Some even stood on their front porch watching as Mom and I drove away. I peered out the window into the darkness wondering if he was watching. The thought of him watching us all that time made me shiver.

Mom kept glancing over at me. It was only a matter of time before she said something. I didn't want to talk. I sat curled up as close to the door as I could.

"Why didn't you tell me, Emma?" Her eyes flashed from the road to me.

I remained silent.

"You know it wasn't your fault." Her voice was soft and caring.

I clenched my jaw. I didn't want to do this. I went through a round of questioning already and was not in the mood to repeat everything.

"You know you can tell me anything." She prodded.

"Mom, stop it!" I yelled, slamming my fists against the dash. "I'm not telling you anything!"

My outburst caused her to flinch. The pained look on her face before she turned to look out her window made me sad.

"I can't right now." Emotion shook my voice as the lump in my throat grew. "I just want to be left alone."

Mom sat in the waiting area as they escorted me off to an exam room. I could only imagine how quick it would spread through the hospital.

Even though I had showered, and probably destroyed any kind of physical evidence he may have left behind, they still wanted me to undergo a whole battery of tests. The scraped under my fingernails for DNA.

They informed me if I had come in within the first twenty-four hours, they could have given me a pill to keep me from getting pregnant, but since it was double that time, they could not offer it. My mind swam. I hadn't given that possibility a thought. Fear gripped me. I closed my eyes fighting nausea that rose out of nowhere. I had to get the trash can, so I didn't get sick all over the floor.

Once alone in the exam room, I battled for control over my emotions and my sanity. The humiliation was almost unbearable. It was all so unfair. I was the one who got violated, and I was the one having to go through all the questioning and physical examination. Nothing happened to him. Hatred burned down deep. I hoped Nick had found this creep and that he paid dearly for what he had done.

Nick's phone vibrated. The caller ID showed it was Andrea. I didn't care. I didn't want to talk to her or anyone else. I turned the power off on the phone and stuffed it into my pocket. If Nick had news, he would have to tell me in person. I didn't want him to see me this way, but I wanted to hear Des suffered. I wanted details; I wanted to hear how he suffered.

I could finally leave with the promise they would have several test results within twenty-four hours. They provided information on rape support groups. How anyone who had this happen to them would want to discuss it with a bunch of strangers was beyond my comprehension. I nodded and pretended to listen while stuffing the papers in a bag and tossing it on the table next to me. I wanted to get away from here.

I avoided eye contact with everyone for fear that just by looking at me they could tell what had happened. Shame once again reared its ugly head.

When we got home, I was reluctant to go back to my room where the nightmare had occurred. It had also been my haven, until they had barged in, now it was turning back into the nightmare. I walked toward my room. Mom followed right behind me.

"Please... I need to do this by myself." I was kind so I wouldn't hurt her feelings.

"Ok, honey. I'll be in the living room if you need me."

I waited until I was sure she had gone before I continued.

Flashes of our skirmish in the hall flew through my mind. I steadied myself running my hand along the wall. I could see my door was open. I stopped before I reached it, unsure of whether I wanted to enter. It seemed so long ago and yet it was fresh in my mind. Holding my breath, I stepped across the threshold and stopped.

Nothing

I stared at my bare mattress. Sounds filled my thoughts first. I covered my ears to keep them out, but they were in my head, burned into my memory banks. I sat Indian style on the floor and squeezed my eyes shut trying to gouge out the scenes that played in front of me.

Anger surfaced. I had to overcome this. He had taken enough away from me. I refused to let him take the ability to be in my room away from me too. I didn't have the strength to make everything go away.

There was a light rap on my door that remained open because it got separated from its hinges when Nick did his shock and awe on it. I opened my eyes trying to get control over my breathing.

Mom stood in the doorway, arms folded across her chest, her eyes red with tears. Even now they threatened to cascade like a waterfall. She managed a small smile. "Nick is here. He's in the den."

I nodded my head, "I'll be there in a minute." I summoned up what little strength I still had left and rose to my feet. I checked my appearance in the mirror and sighed. No fixing or covering up would help. I headed for the den hoping to hear good news.

He was sitting quietly on the couch staring at his hands folded in his lap.

As I walked in front of him, I stared at his fingers hoping to catch a hint of blood, or maybe a cut knuckle; something to show his hunting had not been in vain. There was no evidence of either of those things, but knowing my track record with blood, he would have washed his hands first anyway.

I sat on the opposite end of the couch. "Did you find him?" I kept my eyes locked on his hands.

"Not yet." He held out his hand on the couch in between us.

I stared at it for a moment before I realized what he wanted. I stretched out my arm and placed my hand in his waiting palm. The movement caused more of my arm to show, exposing the bruises that wrapped around my wrist.

He gently ran his thumb over the yellowing coloration.

Minutes passed by as we sat in silence.

His face reflected deep pain. "I don't know what to say, Em. I don't know what to do to make it better."

I clenched my jaw to hold in the anguish that pushed outward from every angle. It was bad enough I was paying for what Des had done, but now Nick too?

"Find him." I took in a sharp breath. "And when you do, make him feel pain; pain and humiliation like I have..." My voice broke as tears fell on the couch.

He reached up and wiped away the tears. More tears replaced them as soon as he dried them.

"Can I hold you?" His voice was strained.

I nodded my head feeling embarrassed that he had to ask. My reaction to him earlier, I was sure, was the reason.

He moved closer and wrapped his big arms around me. The smell of his cologne, and touching his skin, settled my nerves. I felt safe.

"I'm so sorry, Em."

I closed my eyes letting the feeling of security wrap around me. Emotional fatigue was setting in fast. Random thoughts ran through my head. My first experience was not with Nick like I had hoped it would be. It was with this monster instead.

"If only we had done something," I whispered under my breath.

"What?"

"If only we had done something that weekend, Nick."

He pulled back and peered into my face. "What are you talking about?"

I stared at him. "I wish I wouldn't have chickened out that weekend. I wish I would have gone through with it, with you." My facial muscles contracted as I tried to keep the emotion in check.

"That wouldn't have changed anything, Em." He spoke softly as he pushed hair back away from my face. "It wouldn't have stopped this from happening."

"If you would have pushed it, I would have let you. Memories would be of you instead of him!" I grabbed the front of his shirt. "Why didn't you push it? What kind of memory is that for a first time?" I was getting angry again, angry that Nick didn't allow us to be intimate.

He wrapped his arms around me again. "I'm sorry, Em, but if I would have pushed it... how would I have been any different from him?" His breath caught in his throat. "I would never do that to you; I love you." His body trembled with silent sobs.

"I'm sorry." I held on to him desperately wanting his anguish to go away. "I love you too."

He kissed the side of my head and hugged me. I felt strength in his embrace; I tried to draw from it somehow. I felt so weak in every aspect. I grabbed a tissue from the coffee table and offered some to Nick. Seeing his reddened eyes only made it harder for me to get a grip.

"Can you stay awhile?" I asked, dabbing at my eyes.

He smiled his lopsided smile. "I'll stay as long as you want."

Chapter 6

I stayed home a few more days until the bruises were gone. The invisible emotional bruises would far outlast the physical. It relieved me that all my tests came back negative for any kind of sexually transmitted diseases, and the pregnancy test was also negative. Now that the burden of not knowing had been removed, I could take a deep breath.

Everyone watched me as I walked down the hallway at school. Some didn't even wait for me to pass before they whispered to each other. They looked at me with pity, disgust, curiosity, and some were clueless until someone close by filled them in. I averted my gaze from their prying eyes. I focused on the shiny, buffed flooring as I walked from class to class, always aware of their eyes on me. I thought I was just being paranoid, but there were too many instances for it to be a coincidence. How anyone knew I couldn't be sure. I kept to myself and didn't speak to anyone.

The bell and a clap of thunder announced the end of seventh period. Mom was still at work and made me promise that I would ride the bus; there was no way I would do that. I searched my backpack for my umbrella. I had left it on the kitchen table this morning. Maybe I could get home before it rained. I zipped my coat up and headed toward home. We didn't live too far from the school. I figured it would only be about a thirty-minute walk. The wind picked up whipping my hair around my face. I was about a quarter of the way when the rain started. It began as little cold drops of moisture that turned into large

drops of freezing rain. I quickened my pace. The freezing moisture was building up on the sidewalk and it was sticking to my
hair. The coat I had grabbed this morning didn't have a hood,
and I didn't bring a stocking cap or gloves.

I glanced over my shoulder and saw a little black sport car
driving slowly behind me. After a few moments, it still had not
passed me. I looked again. I didn't recognize the car, and the
darkly tinted windows didn't allow extra light in for me to even
try to guess who the driver was. I walked faster. My feet slid
every few steps. My brain was going in a hundred different directions cranking out possibilities I didn't want to think about. My
stomach tied itself in knots.

"Emma, right?"

I ignored the male voice.

The car stopped, but I kept walking. I still wasn't sure who it
was. New thoughts filled my mind. If this person continued to
follow me, it would lead them to my house. Maybe they already
knew where I lived. I decided if they were still following me I
would just walk on to Nick's house and hope that his parents
were home.

"Hey!"

I kept my line of site straight in front of me. The car pulled
even with me.

"It's Casey, from school. We have a couple of classes together."

Casey? My brain registered the information and came up
with a match. Casey was a clean cut guy with short blonde hair,
slim build, and seemed to keep to himself. He knew answers
when called upon in class and he was always on the Honor Roll.
Wow, where that came from I wasn't sure.

He stopped the car. "Can I give you a ride? It's awful cold."

My teeth were chattering so loud he could probably hear
them in the street. I stopped and stood in the cold rain debating.
It was at least another fifteen minutes home. My hair felt frozen,
and my cheeks were feeling the brunt of the windy rain.

He popped open the passenger side door. "Get in, it's okay."

He held out his cell phone. "If it will make you feel better, you can call whoever you want and talk with them all the way." His smile seemed sincere.

What did I have to lose that hadn't already been stolen from me? I got in the car and shut the door.

He turned the heater on high and hit the button to get my window up. "You look half frozen! What on earth are you doing walking in this kind of weather?" He drove along, glancing at me as he spoke.

I rubbed my numb fingers together trying to get the blood flowing and generate heat back into my cold flesh. I didn't bother looking at him as I spoke. "I didn't want to ride the bus."

"I don't blame you," He laughed. "But I think it would be better than this mess."

The car slid. Prepared to slide into the curb, my frigid fingers latched onto the armrest. He corrected it easily as if he did it all the time.

He noticed my stranglehold on his interior and smiled. "I know how to drive in this stuff and my car is a front wheel drive." He looked at the road and then back at me. "I assure you, you're perfectly safe."

I released my grip and put my fingers up to the vent once more. The sting in my flesh told me the feeling was coming back. "Turn right up here and then take a left. My house is the second one on the right."

He pulled into my driveway, put the car in neutral, and pulled the emergency brake.

I pulled my purse onto my lap and grabbed the loop of my book bag. "Thanks for the ride, Casey. I appreciate it."

"Do you walk home all the time?"

I shrugged. I felt awkward being in a car with someone other than Nick. I realized I had never been in a car with a guy except for Nick and Daniel.

"Cause if you do, I can give you a ride. I don't live far from here and it wouldn't be a problem." He rested one hand on the steering wheel and played with the gear shift moving it back and forth.

I sat just staring at the console.

"Okay." He drew out the word and took in a deep breath.

Yeah, right now he probably thought I was mental.

"Do you have a ride to school in the morning?"

"No." I kept my eyes downcast.

"Well, you do now." He slapped the car into reverse, holding the clutch in. "I'll pick you up." He flipped his windshield wipers on high and flooded the windshield with fluid watching the patches of ice break apart. "That is IF we have school tomorrow."

"Thanks." I opened the door and juggled my load getting out. Half way up the sidewalk I hit a slick spot. One foot shot out from under me in one direction, up. Unfortunately, it was the one all my weight was on. My arms flared out trying to gain my balance. I landed hard on my backside. I was sure I would sport a good-sized bruise on my right hip tomorrow. My purse lay upside down in the grass next to me with everything spewing out. Hands tugged at my arms. Memories from the attack rampaged through my thoughts. I screamed and jerked to get away, rolling across the grass. I sat up ready to run.

Casey remained squatted down, his arms positioned to help me up. He stared at me through the frozen cold for a moment before straightening himself. Keeping his hands in front of him in a non-aggressive manner, he walked toward me. "I didn't mean to frighten you."

I tried to get my breathing under control. My backside was feeling the cold wetness of the lawn. "Sorry." I mumbled, wiping the corners of my eyes.

He shook his head. "No, I should have known better."

I squinted my eyes at him. "Is there anybody in this town that doesn't know?" I slapped the ground angrily.

He looked uncomfortable and avoided eye contact with me.

I pursed my lips together, but they trembled anyway.

He took a step forward and held out a hand. "You need to get up off the cold ground."

I grabbed his hand with both of mine. He hauled me to my feet. He returned to where my belongings lay and scooped everything back into my purse.

I stared at him as he held onto my things in one hand and offered me his elbow.

"I'll help you to your door; if that's ok?"

I nodded my head too dumbfounded to do anything more.

He stood at my door until I got it unlocked and threw my things in the foyer.

I felt like I owed him an explanation. I turned and took in a deep breath. "I.."

He shook his head. "It's okay." He walked to his car.

Irritated at my total lack of control, my fingernails dug into the palms of my gripped fists. Here the guy was trying to help me, and I totally freaked out. I chalked that up as one more reason to hate the one jerk responsible for my reaction.

Casey's car sat running in the driveway, driver door still open from where he had sprinted to my rescue. He paused when he got to his car. He offered me a small smile. "I'll see you in the morning." Without waiting for a response, he jumped into the driver's seat, gingerly backed out, and drove away.

I locked the door. Only a few more days and I would see Nick. Thanksgiving was coming up soon, and I was looking forward to spending time with him although my plans over the holiday would be different now.

Casey picked me up as promised and brought me home. And so, the routine began.

He seemed content to talk and let me listen; he didn't push for conversation. In a few short days I felt at ease around Casey. He was turning out to be a good friend. I didn't mention to Nick that Casey was giving me rides. I wasn't sure how the whole guy jealousy thing worked, and I didn't want to set anything off when there was no reason.

Casey and I sat at the old lunch table on the last day before

Thanksgiving break. He toyed with his fries and was not very talkative.

"What's going on?" I squirted ketchup out of the little white packet. The maximum amount of ketchup packets the school allowed you were two. No chance of overdosing on ketchup here.

"What do you mean?" He twirled a fry between his fingers.

"You're not eating and you're not talking." I dunked a few fries in my ketchup and stuck them in my mouth.

He tossed the fry back on his plate. "I've just been thinking about stuff."

"And?" I watched him as I chewed.

He glanced at me for a moment before going back to chasing fries around on his plate. "You just seem really bummed. I wish I could do something to help you feel more... happy."

"Oh." I avoided eye contact with him and poked at the dark, round object the lunch ladies were trying to pass off as a hamburger.

"Not that it's any of my business. I know you've been through some stuff..." He looked up at me. His eyes questioned if it was safe to continue with his thoughts. "Well, I don't blame you. I would probably be the same way. You just need to loosen up a little."

My brain was trying to determine if I should be upset by what he said even though it had some truth to it.

He looked worried. "I hope I haven't offended you. That wasn't my intention." He interjected.

"No, I'm not offended." I swallowed my food. "I'm just not sure how to loosen up. I'm some kind of dweeb, I guess."

"Nah, you're not a dweeb. You just need to get out a little and do some things." He smiled and took a bite of his round, brown blob. "Not wike a date dough." He shoved food back into his mouth that tried to make a getaway.

I laughed more out of embarrassment than how his sentence just sounded. A guy asking me on a date; come on!

Chapter 7

Nick kept his promise and was back home for Thanksgiving, but he would have to go back early for some church outreach. I was just glad he was home even if it was only for a few days.

We ate lunch at his parent's house. It was awkward at first. It was more because of me than them. I was still having trouble adjusting; things were not the same anymore.

Nick, who was a natural-born eating machine, seemed to enjoy himself. It astounded me at the amount of food he ate. He commented that he wouldn't eat again for a month. Apparently in his world a month is a couple of hours because he was back in the kitchen getting another plate.

He said his family had a tradition of stuffing themselves, taking a nap, and then stuffing themselves once more. I believed it to be true. Nick and his Dad were in the front room watching football, each kicked back in a recliner. A few minutes later, they were both snoring away. The adage 'Like father, like son', had just been proved. At one point it seemed they were having a snoring contest to see who could be the loudest. Nick's Dad was winning.

Jenny and Mrs. Edwards recorded them and then played it back to see if they woke up, no response.

When they awoke, we told them the story of the epic snoring. They didn't believe us until we replayed the video for them. Jenny playfully threatened it would make good blackmail material.

We ate dinner at my house with Mom. One drawback of not living close to relatives is that they weren't around for holidays or special occasions. It was quieter at my house.

I stretched out on the couch in the den with my head resting on Nick's leg. He stretched out his big socked feet, resting them on the coffee table. He had his nap earlier, now it was my turn I thought drowsily. We had the fireplace on, and I snuggled in the softest, warmest blanket I could find. It wasn't long and the pattern in his breathing changed. He was sleeping again! I only hoped it would be void of the snoring this time. The fire danced in front of us casting its glow against the shadows on the walls. T.V. sounds drifted in from the other room where Mom was no doubt stretched out. She would have to be at work soon. Maybe the eating and napping thing would become our tradition too. I drifted off into a nice cozy slumber.

Terror interrupted my sleep. I was re-living that night all over again. I knew it had to be a dream, but it felt real. The fear it induced was staggering. I could smell the cigarette smoke and alcohol. I commanded my eyes to open, but they wouldn't co-operate. I felt hands on my body. I pushed and shoved swatting at the air. I couldn't see him there, but I could feel him.

Within minutes it was over, fear and shame lingered behind. Sobs shook my body awake. I surveyed my surroundings through tear-blurred vision. I needed to verify what was going on, that he wasn't here with me. I was on the floor in between the couch and the coffee table.

Nick sat on the floor next to me looking forlorn.

I wiped at my eyes to see more clearly.

"Are you ok?" He questioned, through tear laden eyes.

It took a brief second before I figured it out. I narrowed my eyes at him. "You!"

He looked at me and then over his shoulder as if he expected someone else to be standing there that I was talking to. "Are you awake?" He waved his hand in front of my face.

Inundated with rage and pain I growled at him. "You did it, didn't you?"

"I.."

"I can't believe you did it again." Tears rained down my cheeks. "You told me you would never push me, not that deep!"

I tried to get up, but I was so wrapped up in the blanket I was a mummy from the waist down. "I told you I didn't want to discuss that with you!"

"Here, let me.." He reached for the twisted blanket.

"Get away from me!" I yelled, trying to move away. "Why would you want me to feel like that again? To feel... him." I sobbed. "Why?" I was still working on getting my legs untangled.

"I didn't..." He protested.

Every emotion dumped into my body at once. "Leave!" Anger overflowed into my voice. "Get out!" My body shook. I felt like I might explode into pieces at any moment. I wanted him away from me. I didn't want to remember that night, and I definitely didn't want anyone to force me to recall such unpleasant thoughts. I covered my face with my hands that were as cold as ice. "Please, just leave." I whispered.

He quietly got up, grabbed his shoes, and was out the door.

I rocked back and forth hugging my knees. He knew I didn't want to discuss what happened with anyone; especially him. Shame washed over me in tidal waves. I fought to keep my head above them. It was like having a deep cut, after a little time it has started to heal, a scab forms and then you bump against something ripping the scab off. It reopens the wound all over again, and with the reopening the pain returns! Betrayal and anger choked out every other feeling. How could he do this? I was glad he left!

My thoughts cleared long enough for reality to set in that I had asked Nick to leave. Panic at my reaction tried to settle in my stomach. A little thought appeared out of nowhere. 'No, if he really loved you he wouldn't have made you re-live that horror again to get himself precious information!' It had been a long time since I had felt strength from anger

. It was an old friend, and the reunion was bittersweet. I breathed deeply through my nose, taking control once again over my body and mind. 'Be strong, Emma.' It wasn't Dad's voice, but it gave me strength.

Another thought. 'Let Nick have his church, he loves it more than you, anyway.'

"That's probably right!" I huffed out loud. I stalked off to bed feeling a newfound strength I had never felt before. I couldn't explain how, but it was different.

I turned out the light and lay in bed wondering what it would be like without Nick now. A twinge of fear stabbed through my mind.

'You don't need him, anyway.' Came the thought.

I plugged my new phone in and put it on silent. I pondered if I was going crazy. These thoughts didn't seem to be my own, strength radiated from them. It felt like something inside had snapped, like an old rubber band stretched too far and pops without warning. I yawned and then no more thoughts came, my eyes became too heavy to hold them open.

I awoke feeling great. I had slept like a rock; I couldn't remember the last time I slept so well. Feeling a weird sense of freedom, I took in a deep breath and stretched for my phone. I had to look at the clock twice. It was almost noon. I smiled to myself. There was a text message from Nick. My finger hovered over the button. Should I read it?

'And give him a chance to give you some lame excuse of why he did it, or give you some suck-up apology?'

I stared at his name feeling divided; after all I loved him.

'Yes, loved him. Have you forgotten what he did to you last night? How he dug into your personal thoughts and feelings?'

I watched the screen fade to black. Didn't I owe him a chance to explain?

'You don't owe him anything, especially after what he did!'

I flip-flopped between feeling strong and feeling like a little girl who couldn't help herself and needed someone to take care of her.

'Who do you want to be, someone who can stand on her own or someone who is pitifully weak?'

I was at war with myself. I tossed my phone back onto the

bedside table. A thin layer of dust stared back at me. No sense in living in a pigsty I decided. I rolled out of bed with thoughts of cleaning taking center stage.

I left my phone on silent the rest of the day. I got a couple more texts from Nick and he even tried to call; I ignored them all. The more I ignored him, the stronger I felt. When a thought of Nick or fear of him not being around entered my brain, I kicked it back out. This became easier as the days went on.

I knew Nick had plans with his campus church and since I wasn't taking calls or reading his text; I wasn't even sure when he would come back home. I made sure on the weekends I hung out with Casey away from my house.

Mom asked me once about Nick. I rolled my eyes at her and said it was a long story before quickly exiting the room. Stephanie even tried to talk to me about Nick. I made it clear that I would not discuss Nick with anyone. It was my personal business, and I was going to keep it that way.

I found it odd how comfortable I felt around Casey in such a short amount of time. I didn't think of him as a boyfriend, so maybe that was why. He didn't poke and prod for answers he simply let me be me, whatever that was.

Thanks to Des I had to take finals because I missed over three days of school. Although the school felt badly about the incident that had taken place, they had to adhere to the policy. I was furious, and it gave me one more reason on the growing list of reasons to hate Des even more.

While Casey was helping me study, I fell asleep at least twice. The energy drinks didn't seem to help. Casey cracked a few jokes about me falling asleep. Although I worried about my sleep talking he didn't mention anything about it. Maybe my newfound self didn't do that anymore. What a relief that would be.

After another night of falling asleep, Casey said he would get me something that would definitely keep me awake.

Saturday night he picked me up around dark. We cruised through town with the windows down, heat on full blast, and the music blaring. He pulled into a gas station and parked near the end of the sidewalk that ran in front of the store.

"So, what's on the agenda for tonight?" I asked, looking around. I wasn't familiar with this part of town. Trash lined the curb and the convenience store window had bars over them. Looking further down the street it seemed dark and dangerous; most of street lights were burned out or had been busted out. The houses that ran along the edges of the street looked like they were badly in need of repair. One house had a car in front of it that was missing both the front doors. I had an uneasy feeling about this area. I turned and looked in the opposite direction across the street from where we had just come from, and it was a different world. Every street light was shining brightly on the street; the yards were manicured and perfect. It was as if someone drew a line through these two areas and made one side prim and proper and the other wild and unruly.

Casey shut the car off. "I told you we would get you something to help keep you awake." He craned his neck out the window toward the back of the car. He watched each person who walked by.

"Who are you looking for?"

Casey looked behind us once more. "I'm supposed to meet a guy here."

"Do you know his name silly?" I laughed.

"Kind of."

I was beginning to dislike this idea. The people that were walking by didn't look like very nice people. They reminded me of the people you would see on tv running from the police. I was totally out of my element. Some girls were hanging out over by the corner. Their attire was skimpy considering the temperature outside, and how they walked in heels so high was crazy. I realized maybe this was their night job.

"Let's just go, I'll be ok." I zipped up my hooded jacket as a shiver ran through my body.

He looked at his watch. "He should be here any minute now."

I slid my hand along the armrest and casually locked my door.

Casey laughed at my action. "You're ok." He reached in his pocket and pulled out a wad of cash. He handed me a twenty-dollar bill. "Here, go get us some hot chocolate or something."

I stared at him. Did he really want me to go out there? "You'll be fine, go on."

I grabbed the money and ventured out of the safety of the car. The store wasn't much cleaner than the parking lot. I wandered to the back of the store careful not to make eye contact with anyone. After seeing the uncleanliness of the store, I passed on the hot chocolate. I filled up a styrofoam cup of hot cocoa for Casey. After an unsuccessful search for a lid that fit the cup, I concluded that Casey would have to do without. I turned and headed to the counter ready to get out of there.

A man standing in the corner stared at me. He was dressed similar to the people I had seen walking in and out, but his demeanor was different. He seemed to be looking for something in particular. I was glad I left my purse at home. I stood in line as patiently as I could behind two other people. I looked to the corner again. He was still eyeing me.

I paid and headed for the door keeping the man in my peripheral vision. He pushed himself away from the wall with his elbow and headed toward me. My heart beat sped up. I told myself to calm down; it was just a coincidence he stared at me the whole time, and he happened to want to leave when I did.

I hurried to the car; it was locked. I scanned the parking lot. Casey stood at the other end talking to a guy in a blue baseball cap, baggy jeans and a sweatshirt that looked too big for him. I looked over my shoulder as I hurried to where Casey was, careful not to spill the lava hot drink on my hand.

The guy who had been watching me came out the door, his eyes still glued on me. I was having trouble keeping the lid on my self-control.

At least walking toward Casey, I was walking in the direction of the good side of town; that provided a little comfort.

Casey looked over his shoulder at me and then turned his attention back to the guy in the hat.

"Here." I held the steaming cup in front of him.

He took the cup and set it on the ground by his feet.

I glanced back at the door. The guy was now moving in our direction.

"We need to go." I looked from the man to Casey.

The guy in the ball cap pulled a plastic baggie out of his pocket.

Oh no, this can't be a good thing. "What are you doing Casey?"

He ignored me.

I repeated my question a little more loudly. My demand went unnoticed.

In between glances of the weirdo guy walking our way, I watched Casey and the guy in the cap exchange something for the rolled-up bills Casey had pulled out earlier.

The one who was stalking me broke into a run. "Police!" He shouted. "Stay where you are!"

I shot Casey a look of disbelief. My jaw dropped open so far, my chin could have drug on the ground.

The guy in front of us pulled me to him. He tugged on my front jeans pocket. It happened so fast I wasn't sure what was happening. He ran to our left heading to the back of the store.

A police car flew into the parking lot with lights flashing and sirens blaring.

I stood in the grass like a deer caught in the headlights.

Casey grabbed my hand and jerked me into a run behind him. We ran through the grassy area and jumped a deep ditch that served as a shallow grave for the three-wheeled shopping cart laid over on its side; forgotten and rusting. We ran across the street and through someone's yard.

Footsteps echoed behind us as we fled into the night. Thoughts flashed through my mind of all the television shows of people trying to outrun the cops and how badly they all ended.

Casey was fast, and I had a tough time keeping up with him. We ran through bushes and hedges that ripped my jacket and bit into my arms.

After running through several yards and weaving here and there, we stopped by a huge tree in some stranger's backyard.

"We've got to split up." Casey spouted breathlessly. "I think there was only one after us; odds are better if we go in different directions."

"What?" My thoughts went in a thousand directions. I wasn't familiar with this side of town; how was I going to get home; I didn't even know where I was.

He gulped in some much-needed air. "I'll have one of my friends pick up my car and then get me." He held his breath and peeked around the side of the tree, staring intently in the direction we had just come from. "You find a safe place to hang out, call me and I'll come get you." His chest heaved in unison with mine.

A stream of light about fifty yards away from us lit up part of a backyard. The cop was getting close.

He pointed in the direction away from the law. "You go that way."

Unable to speak, I nodded. The thought I might end up running from the law in the frigid night air had never occurred to me, I now wished I had opted for a lot warmer jacket.

I ran from house to house, using the darkened yards to hide my escape. I stopped and watched behind me for a few minutes. Two houses back I saw the beam light again. How he was trailing me I didn't understand. My heart pounded a little harder.

What if Casey was wrong and there were two cops, one was after him and one after me? Maybe I should just turn myself in. No, I had already run, and that was worse than if I would have just been arrested at the convenience store. The word arrested bounced around my head; what had I gotten myself into? The sound of keys jingling jarred me back to reality. He was closing in. My surroundings were still unfamiliar. I had to make a quick decision on which way to go. I knew one direction I wouldn't be going.

My phone belted out a tune. I jerked it out of my back pocket and pounded on the buttons to make it stop. I glanced at it to see if it was Casey. The caller I.D. told me it was Nick. Of all the times for him to call me!

The dog in the fenced yard beside me barked, blowing my cover. I silenced my phone and then shut it off completely.

Music floated on the chilly breeze. I strained to figure out which direction it was coming from. The neighborhood was nice, so I figured at least I was safer on this side of town. Maybe there was a concert or something and I could get lost in the crowd. I ran in the music's direction, stopping only for a few seconds to make sure I was still headed in the right direction.

The dog barking gave me warning that the cop was hot on my trail now. I could totally understand why the bad people gave up running from the cops, this was getting tiring.

I broke through a row of tall shrubs and found myself in a parking lot filled with cars. The music was a lot louder. A large metal building up ahead had to be where the concert was. I scanned the parking lot making sure it was clear before I broke into a dead run for the front doors. There was no cover out here; if the cop was as close as I thought he was he would have no trouble spotting me.

I slowed as I neared the entrance. The sign read Youth Alive Saturday Night, seven o'clock. I had never heard of that band before. The more youth there was around, the easier it would be for me to blend in. The music was loud so hopefully my late arrival wouldn't be so obvious.
I tried to slow my breathing. I didn't want to draw unwanted attention.

Once inside, I found myself in a large foyer area that was empty. A set of double wooden doors stood straight ahead of me; hallways ran to the left and right. I moved forward a few steps to get a better view of the halls. The one on the right curved around what I guessed was the oval-shaped auditorium just behind the double doors. Doors lined the other side of the hall. I looked down the opposite hall which also curved around. A set of restrooms were close by. I took a few steps intending to hide in the women's restroom, but just because the cop was a guy didn't mean he couldn't go into a women's restroom if they were searching for a, what would I be considered, a druggie, a user, a troublemaker?

I turned and squinted at the glass doors I had entered through, my reflection stared back at me. I squeezed through the double wooden doors. The music hit me full force. It was loud, but not unbearable. I spotted a seat a few rows from the back, on the left side. I sat in the fourth seat from the aisle. I didn't want to sit somewhere that would be an obvious place for someone who might run from the cops.

I quickly jerked my jacket off and tossed it under the chair beside me. I pulled out my pony tail holder and ran my fingers through my hair. I stole glances at those around me. Most of those in attendance were kids my age, mixed in were younger kids and some adults. Some people were sitting, others were standing with arms raised, and several appeared to be crying. My eyes shot to the front up by the stage expecting to see a casket.

The band at center stage jammed out their tune. Small groups gathered in front of the stage. I mimicked a girl two rows up from me and leaned forward, slightly resting my forearms on my legs. My hair hung down hiding my face from any side profile seen from the aisle. I was thankful my breath was back to normal, and I was no longer panting.

I snuck a peek back at the double doors. My heart pounded erratically in my chest. The cop stood a few steps inside the doors, scanning the room from the right to the left. I put my head back down. It would only be a matter of moments before I was busted or free. A sense of dread swept over me. I was subconsciously picking up on some words of the song; something about love and mercy, not getting what I deserved. It dawned on me that I must be in a church service; a weird one that had drums and guitars. I produced a little prayer in my head. 'God, I'm sorry. If you get me out of this, I'll never do anything like this again.' I wasn't sure exactly how prayers worked, but people prayed all the time, so God had to hear them, didn't he? I thought I better throw something in for incentive. 'I'll come to church...' I paused. I didn't want to promise too much so I finished it up with. 'Sometime.'

Any moment now, I thought. I closed my eyes and bit my lip, hoping. I felt someone move up next to me, or maybe it was just my imagination. My palms sweat. I tried to swallow, but there was a large lump in my throat that interfered with the process my throat muscles needed to do to make that happen. I peeked out of the corner of my eye. There was a large pair of tennis shoes next to me. I let my eye wander a little further, there were jeans. Surely the cop wasn't wearing jeans, didn't they have to wear a uniform? I was so scatterbrained I was having trouble keeping any thought.

"He's gone now."

I knew that voice. I jerked my head up and stared.

Nick sat in the padded chair next to me. "If you're wandering about the cop, he left." He wiped his nose with a tissue and then stuck it in his pocket. His reddened eyes stared straight ahead, his face emotionless.

I hadn't seen him since I asked him to leave a few weeks ago. I hadn't answered his text or calls. I felt about an inch tall. I tried to think of something to say. Feelings surfaced that I had successfully pushed down.

He sighed. "Come on, I'll take you home." Without another word he got up and walked out.

I trailed behind him. The frigid air reminded me I was minus one jacket. I was not about to go back into that church or whatever that building was. The car was just as cold as the outside. I tried to keep my body still. The shivering took control against my will.

Nick stripped off his sweatshirt and handed it to me. His

muscled physique was visible beneath his form fitting long-sleeved shirt. I pulled it over my head, the smell of his cologne made me dizzy with memories. The material was warm with his body heat. A longing surfaced, I shoved it back down and ran the thoughts out of my head. "Thank you." I rubbed my hands together to generate heat.

The ride home was quiet. I stole quick glances at him trying to figure out what was going on in his head. His expression gave me no clue. He pulled up in my driveway. I expected him to shut the car off and to want to sit and talk like we had done so many times before, but things were different now. I sat waiting for him to say something. The silence was worse than him being mad, or cussing me out, or yelling, or something, anything.

"I need to get back." He seemed to want to say more, but he held his tongue.

The compassion in his eyes confused me, he should be furious with me. After the way I treated him, ignored him, I didn't deserve his compassion. I broke eye contact and looked at the darkened house. I forgot Mom had to work tonight. I hesitated, maybe I should ask him to take me somewhere else; but where? I hadn't been in touch with Stephanie in a while. What would she think if I showed up on her doorstep without warning?

"Would you like me to go in with you and check the house?"

I looked from the house to him fighting back tears; tears of fear, of frustration, of the unknown. I tried to shake the feeling.

He put the car in park and shut the engine off. "Come on, I don't mind." He opened the door and climbed out.

As I walked to the door, my eyes darted everywhere, to every corner of nearby houses, searching the darkest parts of yards, around cars, looking for any sign he might be near.

I felt silly as Nick turned on every light, searched every closet, under the beds, anywhere someone might hide, including the garage. He even made sure every window and door were locked. We walked back to the foyer.

"Thanks, Nick." I took in a breath. "I'm sorry you had to come in and..."

"It's okay, Emma."

Every nerve ending in my body jumped at the sound of his voice saying my name. I stared at his chest as emotions swirled in a whirlpool around my heart.

He put his hand on my arm and smiled. "I'll see you around. Take care."

Old feelings fluttered within.

He turned, unlocked the door and had one foot on the front porch when he paused.

My heart leapt in my chest as he turned back. Maybe he would say something about us; I looked at him eagerly.

He smiled again and shook his head staring at the floor. "I know this will sound really weird." He cocked his head sideways. "But I feel like..."

I was almost leaning toward him in anticipation.

"I feel like God wants me to tell you... that you owe him one." He shook his head again. "I hope that makes sense." He shut the door and was gone.

I locked it and watched him through the front room window. He ran his fingers through his hair still shaking his head. Did God really hear my prayer?

I retreated to my bedroom and locked the door for the night. I stared into the darkness for a long time pondering about the prayer and about God.

Out of nowhere it popped into my head that I had shut my cell phone off. I was supposed to call Casey! I scrounged around in the dark until I found my jeans and pulled my phone from my back pocket. I had several text messages from Casey wanting to know where I was. I felt terrible for not getting back to him. I sent a text I was home safe, and I would talk to him later.

I grabbed my jeans to throw them in the hamper. I felt a lump in my front pocket. I pulled out a plastic bag. I used the light from my phone to inspect the contents. Inside the plastic bag were several little baggies filled with different pills. Some were capsules and others were round or oblong and assorted colors. I thought the guy in the baseball cap tried to get something out of my pocket; it never dawned on me he was putting something in.

I stood in my bedroom stunned. I had no idea what these pills were. If Mom saw them, she could probably tell me the name of every single one, what each one was for, and why to take them. She would also want to know where I got them. That was one story I didn't want to tell. I shoved them under my mattress for safe keeping. I would get rid of them first chance I got. I finally nodded off after I heard Mom come home around seven.

Some nights were better than others when I was alone in the house. Nick had made a complete search of the house and no one was there but fear still lingered. Sometimes I could feel him lurking outside trying to find ways in.

I dreamt about the void. This time I was in the meadow alone, Nick wasn't there. The dream always started out pleasant and ended up badly. I knew what to expect when the dark clouds moved in and the wind picked up. Hopelessness consumed me. I couldn't find anything to make the void go away or even just satisfy it. I lay on the ground writhing in pain as the void grew bigger.

Across the meadow someone walked in my direction. As the figure grew closer, I could see it was a man dressed in white. His face was bright. I held up my hand to block the brightness; it was no use. As he drew closer, instead of him blocking the sun, it was like it shone through him, keeping his identity hidden.

"It will be all right." His voice brought instant peace.

The void was still there, but with him beside me it didn't grow.

I opened my eyes. I was safe in my bedroom. The peace I felt in my dream remained with me. I took in a deep breath, enjoying the absence of fear, worry, and shame. A feeling of love washed over me nearly bringing me to tears.

Chapter 8

Casey and I didn't discuss what happened that night in the parking lot except that it would NEVER happen again.

School finals didn't turn out to be as bad as I thought. Casey had drilled me with all the studying, and I thought I did well.

It was Friday night. Snow was in the forecast, just in time to kick off the winter holiday. The first snow of the season always excited me.

Casey picked me up, and we headed to his friend's house to hang out for the evening. A handful of people were already there when we arrived. We had the basement to ourselves. They provided snacks for us to munch on and some punch. The guys got involved in a poker game that lasted for hours. I sat listening to the other girls talk about their boyfriends. One girl named Leslie thought me and Casey were together. I cleared that up quickly and excused myself to get more punch; it was the best I ever tasted.

As the night wore on the girls grew funnier. Everything was cracking me up. I was on my way to get more punch when I stumbled and somehow ended up in the lap of one of the guy's sitting at the table. I couldn't quit laughing.

"I think we better head out now." Casey smiled as he assisted me off the guy's lap.

The chilly air outside seemed to straighten me up a little. "Sorry, I don't know what happened back there." I struggled to fasten my seatbelt.

Casey rescued me and hooked the belt with ease. "I think you've had a wee little too much to drink."

I frowned at him. "I haven't been drinking."

He laughed as we drove away from the house. "What do you

think was in the punch?"

I thought for a minute. "Fruit juice and lemon, lime pop stuff." My brain wasn't functioning right.

"Yeah, but there was a little something extra in there too."

"Alcohol?" My voice boomed in the car. "Sorry." I whispered.

Casey shook his head smiling. "I can't take you home like this, that's for sure."

"I don't like alcohol. Are you sure there was alcohol?" I reached for my purse and totally missed it. I sighed.

We pulled up to a fast food restaurant. Casey opened his door. "I'll go get you some food; that should help."

I waved at him through the window and made a face just having fun. I got out of the car thinking maybe the freezing air might do me good and waited.

He soon returned with some food. I took a couple of bites and quit.

"I'm not hungry. My stomach feels sloshy." I scratched my head. "Is that even a word; sloshy?" I giggled. "Sloshy." I repeated it using my deep voice.

Casey chuckled, "You're toasted!"

"Toasted sloshy!" I fell against the car. "Oh!" My laughter echoed across the parking lot.

Casey helped me to stand up straight. I didn't like the look in his eye. I found myself trapped between him and the car. He looked like he was going to...

He leaned forward and kissed me.

I tried to pull away and lost my balance. He leaned against my body wedging me even more between himself and the car.

I shook my head, "I don't want..."

"Shhh." His hands cupped my face as he kissed me again.

"I don't want to do this." I pushed him away a few inches, but he came right back.

"I really don't care what you don't want." He scowled at me. "I've invested a lot of time in you, and I hate to invest in something without getting a return."

"No." I turned my head, fighting the sick feeling that rose to the top of my throat. I closed my eyes for a moment thinking it might help me feel better. I tried to push him away; I wanted to push him away, but my body was not cooperating with the directions my brain was sending.

"Hi, Emma."

I swung my head around trying to get my vision to stop wobbling and squinted. "Nick?"

"This is none of your business." Casey turned my head back to face him. "Come on, I'll take you back to my house."

"No. I...I don't wanna go to your house." I shook my head.

Casey opened the door and shoved me hard onto the seat of the car. "Come on, we're leaving!"

"I believe she said no." Nick grabbed the door with one hand and kept it open.

"Back off man!" Casey tried to shut the door.

I managed to get my legs out of the car but couldn't quite get the momentum needed to get my rear out of the seat. "I don't want to go." The slur in my speech alarmed me. How many cups of punch did I have, three, four? Too many, I guessed.

Nick pushed Casey away from the door.

Jasper's head popped in the car. "Need help?"

"Hi! How are you?" I sounded way too bubbly. I shoved both my arms in front of me for assistance.

Nick and Casey were arguing.

Jasper had his arm around my back holding me up as he pulled me out of the car.

"You're strong." I giggled.

Jasper smiled politely. "Yep."

"You're not going to take her anywhere, at least not tonight!" Nick squared off with Casey.

"She is going with me!" Casey glared back.

Nick kept his eyes targeted on Casey. "You're not very smart if you push this."

Casey laughed sarcastically. "I'm not very smart? To hear her tell it," He pointed his finger at me. "You're the one who pushed a little too far."

I wagged my head back and forth; feeling the weight of my skull. My control over my body was getting worse. "I didn't say anything to you, Casey; I didn't say anything to anybody." I tried to take a step, luckily Jasper had my back literally, or I would have been eating asphalt.

"I must say, the whole 'sleep talk' thing, can come in pretty handy." Casey raised his eyebrows at Nick. "But I guess you already know that."

Nick took a threatening step forward. "That's enough."

"Oh, I've just started." He scoffed. "I've learned some very interesting things lately."

"Casey, what are you saying?" I felt the tip of his knife in my back but hoped he wouldn't sink it in further. If he knew about the sleep talking, what else did he know? Things started to spin.

"Sorry, babe. I know you said you still loved Nick," He chuckled. "But tonight, I'll give you what he wouldn't." He turned and walked toward me. "So, let's head back to my house."

"I said enough!" Nick bellowed.

"What?" I looked at Jasper trying to hold my head still. "What's he talking about?"

Jasper shrugged, but I knew exactly what he was talking about. I felt embarrassed that Casey knew Nick had turned me down; I was probably the only one he ever turned down. I was angry, but I wasn't sure who I was angrier with, Nick or Casey.

Nick nodded at Jasper. "Take her to the truck"

"Come on Nick, you had your chance and blew it, let me have mine." Casey cocked his head at Nick and smiled. "How about we take turns?" His laugh was cold and uncaring.

Nick tightened his hands into fists. "I warned you."

"Stop it Casey! I thought you were my friend!" Talking and walking at the same time was not a feat I could accomplish. "Why?" Jasper was ushering me to the truck, but I wasn't finished yet. "Why are you doing this?" I cried angrily.

"Get her out of here, Jasper!" Nick roared.

Jasper swept my feet out from underneath me with one

swoop of his arm. He escorted me, against my will, away from the situation that was quickly developing.

Hot tears rolled down my cheeks as I sobbed into Jasper's neck. "Am I a bad person?"

"No." He answered softly, "You're just... lost."

"Lost? What do you mean?" I stared at him, only there was more than just one of him now.

"I'll explain to you later when..." He paused and then smiled. "When you're a little more yourself."

I tried to wipe the tears off his neck and noticed that more were dropping onto his shirt and jacket.

My third attempt to climb into the truck landed me across the front seat with the bottom half of my body still hanging out. My feet wiggled in the air void of anything to push on to get me further into the truck.

Jasper tried to give me instruction, but it was all mumbled together. He finally helped me, rather awkwardly, scoot over so he could climb behind the wheel.

I leaned against him to keep myself from sliding down into the floor. The vehicle moved and then we stopped. I vaguely knew of the door opening and shutting. I slumped to the other side as we turned a corner. I fell against something firm. I recognized the cologne; it was Nick. I was angry, hurt, disappointed, and relieved all at once. I grabbed onto his hooded sweatshirt. I wanted to be angry but ended up sobbing into it instead.

Chapter 9

I was freezing. I groped around for the covers and pulled them up to my chin, shivering. After a few minutes my brain flooded with all kinds of things that were wrong, the pillow, the blankets, the firmness of the bed, and that it was freezing.

My eyes felt puffy, swollen and sore. I opened them slowly and realized this was not my room at all, but I recognized it. Questions ran through my mind. Why was I in Nick's room; why was I in Nick's bed; and most importantly, where was Nick?

I lay still listening, maybe he was off in another part of the house. The sound of steady breathing filled the air, and it wasn't mine. I peered over the side of the bed. He lay sprawled out on the floor using his arms for a pillow. A throw covered part of his body. I studied him looking for any answers that might present themselves. He looked comfortable in just his jeans. He had undoubtedly adapted to the arctic temperatures that were maintained at his house. His right shoulder had scrapes and scratches. His left hand looked scraped and either it was bruised or dirty; it was hard to tell. Did he get in a fight? Did I do it? I realized he was watching me.

"Good morning." His voice was always deeper when he first woke up.

I missed that. I quickly pushed that feeling away.

"Yeah." I was quickly getting agitated with myself. I couldn't remember what happened last night. How did I get here, and where was Casey?

"How are you feeling?" He rolled over on his side watching me intently.

His chest was as muscular as I remembered. I suppressed more feelings. His lip looked swollen. I couldn't give his lips much thought; it wasn't safe to dabble there. I needed to get out.

"Fine." I threw back the covers. If I was out all night, I would be dead meat.

"I wouldn't do that if I were you." He smirked.

I glared back at him. "Well, you're not me."

Nick was already in motion as I rolled off the edge of the bed and stood. Dizziness hit me like a tidal wave making my knees buckle. I fell into his waiting arms.

He chuckled. "I may not be you, but I've been where you're at, several times."

He lowered me into a seated position back down onto the bed.

The room was spinning now and with that came nausea.

"The room spinning?"

I nodded my head and wished I wouldn't have moved.

"Feeling a little sick?"

"M-huh."

"Mouth feels like you have cotton in it?"

I ran my tongue around my mouth. "Uh-huh."

"Pounding head ache?"

My head was hurting. "What is this, twenty questions?" I moaned. Maybe if I would have stayed in bed, I would have felt better.

"Sit still, I'll be right back." He disappeared into the hallway.

I was no longer freezing, now I was sweating. I moved back on the bed and felt like I would fall over; my equilibrium was not working properly.

Ok, get a grip and remember. I tried to remember coming here to Nick's house with no luck. I backed up further. The last thing I remembered clearly was leaving the party. The punch! It had alcohol in it. I couldn't remember how many cups of it I had ingested, but apparently it was way too much.

Nick returned with a cup in his hand. "Here, drink this."

I took the cup, but after looking in it and smelling it, I offered it back to him scrunching up my nose.

He pushed it back in my direction. "You need to drink it."

"It smells gross!"

"Drink it!" He responded forcefully.

I sighed.

"Trust me." He prodded more gently.

I put it to my lips and sipped it. "Ugh!" I held the glass cup out for him to take it.

"You have to drink it really fast, all at once."

I shook my head. I felt terrible, and I was sure this wouldn't help me any.

"Do you want to feel better or not?" He stood with arms crossed against his chest. Some scars stared back at me. I pushed more thoughts aside.

"Come on, Emma. Trust me, it will help." There was a gleam in his eye that made me cautious, but I gritted my teeth and put the cup back up to my lips. I squeezed my eyes shut and gulped every last drop.

"Here." He held out a wastebasket.

"What's that for?"

He smiled. "You're gonna need it."

I frowned at him. Then it hit me. Whatever that stuff was that I drank was coming back up, and with a vengeance! I grabbed the basket and hurled so hard I thought I might see my socks when I was finally able to open my eyes. I was thankful it had a liner in it; that would have been a mess to clean up.

Nick had disappeared again. If he came back with more of that stuff, I was going to throw it on him. I set the basket down between my feet in case I needed it again.

He reappeared, no cup this time.

"Why did you do that to me?" I snapped at him.

"Don't you feel better?"

I thought for a moment. I felt a little better, but I wasn't going to admit that to him.

"I set out a new toothbrush and some paste if you would like to brush your teeth. There's also a washcloth on the counter and some soap if you want to freshen up a little."

I glanced down at the can and made a face.

"Don't worry about that, I'll take care of it." He moved it over to the side. He stood in front of me and held out a hand. "Need help?"

His kindness was too much. "No, I'll be ok." I said in a small voice.

He dropped his hand and allowed me room.

This time I got up a little more slowly. It was better. I made my way to the bathroom and cleaned up a little. It felt good to wash my face and my arms. I was feeling a lot better. My head still hurt a little, and I was thirsty.

When I got back to Nick's room, he had a little tray on the end of the bed with some dry toast, a hot cup of coffee and a small jar of water with miniature pink roses in it. I had to look away and bite my lip to hold back emotion. I didn't understand why he was being so kind to me. I hadn't given him the time of day in weeks.

"You might want to just sip the coffee. I wouldn't suggest chugging anything for a little while, no matter how thirsty you are; more than likely it would give you the effect you felt last night."

I rubbed my forehead. "Yeah, I don't want that again." I grabbed a piece of toast and nibbled on it. I sat on the edge of the bed and stared at the carpet.

"Do you remember anything from last night?"

I kept my eyes on the floor. "Not really. I remember drinking punch at a friend's house." I looked at him for a moment. "I didn't know it had alcohol in it." I took little bites of the crusty bread.

He eyed me. "You don't remember what happened later?"

I swallowed and shook my head, hesitating. "Did I do something?" I remembered his shoulder and his swollen and busted lip. "Did I scratch your back; did I hurt you?"

"No." His expression gave nothing away. I waited for him to volunteer information, my wait was in vain.

"How did I get here?"

"I brought you here around midnight."

"Why?"

"Because the guy you were with turned out to be a jerk." He leaned against his door frame and crossed his arms.

I put the toast down. "Casey is nice."

"Well, he wasn't last night."

I tried to remember, but there was nothing. I couldn't imagine Casey not being a gentleman. He had never given any indication of being someone other than just that. "I think you're just jealous."

Nick shrugged. "Trust me, he wasn't being very nice."

"Trust you?" I scoffed, "You just gave me something that made me puke my guts up after saying to trust you." I stood up and looked for my shoes. "Is that what happened to your face and your hand, Casey not being nice?" I seethed. "I thought Christians didn't fight!"

"I was defending your honor." He countered.

"Honor?" I laughed bitterly. "What honor?" Tears burned my eyes. "What honor do I have, Nick?"

"You don't remember the things he said to you, do you?" He cocked his head as though he couldn't believe I was defending Casey. He straightened and stuck his hands in his pocket. "Why would I lie to you, Emma?"

"Because you're jealous!" I ranted.

"Do you remember seeing Jasper last night?" He asked calmly.

No memories I could recall. "No."

"Well, he was there, and he saw what happened." He handed me my shoes. "Why don't you call him and ask what happened?"

I sat on the end of the bed and pulled one shoe on. I jerked my shoestrings tight.

There was an awkward silence.

"Are you okay now?" There was a gentleness in his tone.

"What do you mean?" I growled. I tied my other shoe.

He stood in front of me still speaking softly. "You cried a lot last night."

I didn't answer him. That would explain my eye condition. I

was busy searching my brain for any hint that what he was saying was true.

"I think you finally quieted down about four."

I finished with my shoe and glared up at him. "What did you do to make me cry this time; more dabbling into my sleep talk?"

He looked hurt.

Okay, maybe that wasn't fair. I chalked it up to being mad. I had no memory of the things he was telling me. If it was all a ploy to get me to come back to him, it wouldn't work.

"No, Em. It wasn't anything I did." He looked sad.

"Well?" I asked perturbed.

He stared at me for a moment with those brilliant blue eyes. "Last night you remembered the things Casey said to you; what he wanted to do. You said you thought he was your friend." He broke eye contact with me. "I'm sorry he didn't turn out to be the friend you thought."

My breath caught in my throat. No! It was a lie! I stood and grabbed my jacket heading for the door.

He caught my wrist as I walked by. "Where are you going?"

I turned and shook my head at him. I wasn't going to tell him anything.

He loosened his hold. "I told your Mom I would bring you home in the morning."

I sighed. "How am I going to explain this to her?"

"There was no way I was going to take you home in the condition you were in, so I called your Mom and told her you and I were talking about some stuff. I told her you fell asleep, and that I didn't want to disturb you." He released my wrist. "I asked if you could stay and I would bring you home in the morning."

"And she said yes?" I looked at him suspiciously.

"After I told her my parents were home, she said it was fine." He walked to his dresser, chose a shirt, and slid it on over his head.

"Your parents are here?" I asked in a hushed voice. "Did they...", Oh this could be bad. "Did they see me like that last night?"

He grabbed a pair of socks out of another drawer and pulled them on. "They were in bed when we got here last night. They went Christmas shopping early this morning and will be gone all day, so I figured you could recuperate here."

I closed my eyes. How were things getting so messed up over one simple, stupid mistake? Why didn't they tell me the punch had alcohol? If I wouldn't have drunk the punch, I would remember what happened. A tear slipped down my cheek. I quickly wiped it away and wiped my eyes to keep more from falling.

Nick was watching me. He got up and stood in front of me. His eyes penetrated my thoughts. He cupped my cheek with one hand using his thumb to wipe the corner of my eye.

I wanted so badly to give in to my weakness, to fall into his arms weeping, to feel his comfort again like before. He always made everything all right. I swallowed hard, holding back feelings, emotions, and desires that were scratching inside to be set free. I broke eye contact and backed away. "I can't." I whispered. "I need to be strong."

"No, Em. No, you don't." He moved forward and wrapped me in his arms. "I still love you."

A shudder rolled through my body. The dam was cracking. I had to get away, or it would sweep me along when it broke. I pushed him away. "Please." I took in a ragged breath. I held my arm out to keep him from coming too close. "I can't."

"Okay," He countered softly. "Okay."

I watched as he slipped his shoes on, concentrating on anything other than my current emotional state.

He grabbed his keys and wallet from the nightstand. "Let me take you home."

Chapter 10

As soon as we pulled into the driveway, I bailed out of the car. I didn't want to think of things I may have told him last night in my drunken stupor. I needed to get away from him. He was a weakness I couldn't afford to let in; it would mean destruction from the inside out.

I avoided Mom and went straight to my room, locking my door behind me. I sent a text to Casey to get to the bottom of this mess.

'man what a night.. i guess.. can't remember a lot. hope i wasn't too much of a pain.. What time did u drop me off in case my mom asks'

Sitting on the edge of the bed, I stared at the dark blue comforter waiting for a response. Nick wouldn't lie, but how did I end up at his house if he wasn't telling the truth. What did Casey say that freaked me out? I racked my brain for answers that remained hidden. Was there a way I could induce my memory?

I could still smell Nick's cologne on my clothes. Memories came flooding back. Be strong, I told myself. I pushed them out of my thoughts and headed for the shower. It occurred to me that maybe being around Casey would jog my memory.

When I got out of the shower there was still no response from Casey. I sent another text, 'guess it was bad enough you won't even talk to me now huh?'

Within minutes my phone beeped.

I snatched it up expectantly. The message was from Nick. I stared at it hesitant. I hadn't read any of the many texts he had sent me since that night I asked him to leave, and I hadn't answered his calls. I also ignored anything from Stephanie and Daniel. I took in a deep breath and let it out. I guess if what he had said was true about last night he had kept me out of trouble with Mom, and I owed him one. I pulled up the message and read it slowly.

'I am sorry things are so rough for u right now. If u ever need me, I will always be here for you. All my love. Nick.'

Another beep interrupted my thoughts, this one was from Casey.

'You were about three sheets to the wind last night. Lol. You didn't do anything wrong besides giggling about everything.'

Well, that didn't give me the information I was looking for. I was debating on sending another text when my phone sounded off again.

'I dropped you off at around midnight. Want to hang out tonight? No punch though ok? Lol. '

I chewed a fingernail. If Nick was telling the truth, and he took me to his house around midnight, then how could Casey have brought me home at midnight?

'sure'

'Pick you up at 7'

There was a knock on my door.

"Yeah?"

"Is everything ok?" Mom sounded concerned. "Nick said you were upset last night."

"It's ok."

"Are you sure honey, if you want to talk,"

"Everything is fine." I interrupted her.

"Ok."

I knew she was still outside my door, and I wasn't in the mood to be probed with questions.

"I'm going to finish up some Christmas shopping." She paused. "Do you want to come with me?"

I recognized that tone. It was the 'I don't want to appear to be begging you to go, but I really am', tone. She didn't use it often, and she knew I would give in because of it. It Christmas Eve tomorrow, and I hadn't gone shopping for Mom yet. I didn't have any money, anyway.

"How long are you going to be gone? I'm supposed to hang out with Casey tonight."

"However long you want." She sounded more chipper already.

I bit my lip. "I'll be out in a few minutes."

"Ok, I'll put my coat on." I could hear the smile in her voice.

My heart wasn't really into shopping. I tried to make the most of it for Mom as we went from store to store. The items she had in the basket she hid under her coat and made me turn the other way while she paid for them. I found a few things for her, which I had to beg the money for.

I put my plan of getting a job last summer on hold when the attack happened. I didn't have the money for college I thought I would have by now either.

When we left the store, the air outside had turned colder. I could smell the snow; it was just a matter of time.

We hit a couple of more stores buying a few items at each one. As we were leaving the last store, it began to snow big heavy flakes. It lightened my mood some, and I was thankful for that. I listened to Mom go on about her childhood. Stories I could probably recite from memory, but I didn't want to ruin her fun. I hadn't seen her smile this much in a long time. It had been a long year for both of us.

When we got to the house, Mom's mood was in full holiday swing. She had put out a few Christmas decorations and now she wanted to get the tree down from the attic and string popcorn by the fireplace. My mind went back to years past when Dad was here. I was always so excited to help him string popcorn. He would put the popcorn on the needle and I strung it all the way to the end of the thread. When I would break one on accident, he would tell me to hurry and eat it. There were times I broke them on purpose just to get a little popcorn.

"Casey is picking me up in an hour. I don't think I can help this year."

Her smile disappeared. She stood awkwardly holding some Christmas tinsel she had scrounged up from somewhere.

I sighed.

"No, it's ok." She wound the tinsel back up. "Be with your friend." She looked out the window at the snow that was already covering the ground. "Just be careful and be home early in case it gets bad." She disappeared into the other room.

I stared out the window. I wanted change, and I had surely gotten it on every side of my life. The only thing left would be for Dad to show up on the doorstep, and the likelihood of that happening was nil.

I felt terrible thinking about Mom being here all by herself putting up decorations for a holiday about families and her not having any family around. Nanny and Papaw were too old to make the trip to our house because we lived so far away, and things had been a little crazy this year, so Mom mailed gifts instead of delivering them in person. We hadn't had the family at our house for Christmas in such a long time. I knew it must be hard on Mom.

I made a decision. I sent Casey a text telling him I wouldn't be hanging out with him tonight, and we would have to get together after Christmas. I put on a smile, tried to find some holiday pep, and headed off to the kitchen to start the popcorn. Dad was the one missing out, not us.

When Mom reappeared, I told her I was staying home to help her.

"Oh, good." She bit her lip.

I knew that look too well. I narrowed my eyes at her. "What's going on?"

She smiled uncomfortably. "I... well; you weren't going to be here, and..."

"Out with it, Mom!" I demanded playfully.

"I asked Nick to come over and help!" She gave me a grimaced smile.

I pursed my lips together.

"I'll call him and tell him never mind, that you're staying."

The doorbell chimed.

She put her hand on my shoulder. "I'll tell him you decided to stay, and I don't need help after all." She turned to leave.

"No, Mom. It's okay."

She paused in the foyer. "Are you sure? He's a nice boy, I'm sure he would understand."

"Yeah, I'm sure." I was sure my heart was going to be ripped out of my chest and stomped on. I tried to summon up strength. The microwave sounded off in the kitchen and saved me at least a few minutes of being subjected to his muscular, good looks. I shook my head; stop it! I started another bag of popcorn and looked for a large bowl. I went to the big cabinet and quickly realized I had cleaned all that out and moved stuff around. I searched other cabinets and found a bowl on the top shelf. I stretched up on my tiptoes and got part of a fingertip on it, but not enough. I tried again, no luck. I growled at myself for being so short.

"Easy there, tiger." Nick grabbed the bowl and held it toward me.

I snatched it out of his hand.

"You're welcome. Anything else I can help you with? I'm at your disposal."

I turned around intending to sneer a remark, but the words caught in my throat. He disarmed me with his lopsided smile. He had on his red and white striped polo shirt. He looked fantastic tonight; but of course, I couldn't remember when he didn't look good. Even when he was hot and sweaty from mowing yards, he still looked good. I felt my face flame up.

He raised an eyebrow at me. His grin turned into a smirk.

I got my senses back about me. "You look like a candy cane." I turned and rolled my eyes. If that was the best I could come up with, it would be a long night.

His laugh filled the kitchen.

I missed that sound. My throat tightened. I had to get out of there. I took off to my bathroom. I stayed in there for a few minutes trying to get myself together. I couldn't stay in the bathroom all night. Where was that anger I had? That is where my strength came from before. I went back to that night in the den, how I felt. At first it was pain, but then the anger came. I held my head up high and walked into the den where we always put the tree.

Nick was finishing putting the top of the tree on. Mom straightened out the artificial limbs. We had decided a long time ago that an artificial tree was better, no pine needles to worry about dragging through the house, and we didn't have to go out into the cold and fight the crowds to get a good tree.

"I'll get the popcorn!" Mom exited the room with a big smile on her face.

Christmas music filled the air.

Mom was humming as she came back into the room.

I would set aside my differences, for Mom's sake. We laughed, decorated, and snacked on chocolate chip cookies Mom whipped up. The snow was piling up outside. We already had a couple of inches. Maybe we would have a white Christmas this year.

When the decorating was done, we sat around the fireplace with the Christmas lights on and sipped hot cocoa.

Mom's eyes flickered between me and Nick. "I think I will turn in for the night. I'm not as young as I used to be." She winked as she got up. "Merry Christmas to you and your family, Nick."

"Thank you, Ms. Parker. Merry Christmas!"

I took the cups to the kitchen and loaded them in the dishwasher. When I came back into the den, Nick had disappeared. I stood staring at the fire trying my best to fight off memories and feelings that threatened to weaken my armor. I felt him behind me. I ignored him, trying to pull strength from the anger inside, but it was nowhere to be found now after all the joking and laughing.

"If there is anything I have ever done to offend you," His voice was soft and caring.

I whispered inwardly to myself to be strong.

His arms came over my shoulders with something dangling down between his hands. "Or anything I've done to hurt you, I'm sorry." He was trying to fasten a necklace around my neck.

"Can you move your hair?"

"Nick," I sighed. "I don't want anything..."

"Please?" He begged softly.

I felt like I would be sick from the emotion that was choking me. I reached up and moved my hair. I was so torn, and I hated it. He moved and stood in front of me staring at the trinket he had given me. I held it between my fingers. Several little diamonds outlined the shape of a heart.

I shook my head. "You didn't need to get me anything."

"Shh!" He scolded. "Let me explain."

I stared at his chest not wanting to hear what would come next. I already felt the ache in my throat that happened before the tears came. I felt his eyes on me, but I couldn't bring myself to look at him.

"It seems like a long time ago when I told you that only one person has ever held my heart."

My bottom lip trembled. I fought for composure.

"That one person was you, Em."

My heart pounded at the sound of the nickname he had given me. My breaths came a little faster.

"It still is you."

I clenched my jaw as I stared at the heart shape I held in my fingers.

"This is my heart I am giving to you," He gently took the heart from my fingers and pressed it against my chest. "I would prefer that it stay here next to your heart, but it is no longer mine. Do with it what you think is best." His voice choked with emotion. "I will always love you, Em." He cupped my face in his hands and kissed my forehead, then the end of my nose.

My breath had been sucked out of me. My lips were eager against my will.

"No matter what." He finished.

He rested his forehead against mine.

Inside I was screaming out to take hold of him, to tell him I was his forever too, but I couldn't get my body to cooperate. I stood immobile.

He dropped his hands and turned away.

Unable to do anything else, I closed my eyes.

Then he was gone.

I stood motionless as I argued with myself. Part of me wanted to jerk the necklace off and give it back to him to prove I was strong, but another part longed for him desperately. The void grumbled reminding me that not even Nick had satisfied that gaping hole in my life.

I left the necklace on when I went to bed. I found solace in a part of him being here with me. I didn't sleep well and was awake when Mom left for work at six. She tried to work as many days as possible, so I wouldn't be alone at night.

It was Christmas Eve. I opened my blinds and stared at the twinkling lights outside. Our house was the only one on the block that didn't have a flashing extravaganza in the front yard.

I tried hard to get in the Christmas spirit, I couldn't seem to pull it off. A cloud of depression rained down, drowning out any happiness that threatened to show its face. There wasn't much snow accumulation last night. It was nice that it was at least white outside. More snow was in the forecast for the next couple of days.

I sighed as I lay in bed. I didn't feel like getting up. I couldn't think of a good reason to get up. I stayed in bed the rest of the day dozing off and on, staring at the ceiling in between my cat naps. Mom thought I might be getting sick and insisted I eat. I still had my warm pajamas on from the night before. I didn't see a reason to change since bedtime was right around the corner, anyway. Mom and I sat in the living room watching the television. Every time she would reach for her glass she glanced in my direction; a look of worry plastered on her tired face.

"Why don't you take a shower? It might make you feel better." She offered a sympathetic look.

I sighed angrily.

She placed her hand on my forehead. "Well, you don't feel like you're running a fever. I'll go get the thermometer to be sure."

I got up from the chair. "I'll go take a shower! I'm not sick, Mom!" I snapped back at her. I wanted to be alone.

Thoughts and memories ran through my mind unchecked with no emotional reaction to them. I might as well be seeing a stranger's life. I stood in the shower letting the water run until it got cold. I toweled off and stared at myself in the mirror void of any feeling or emotion. Maybe Nick had triggered something inside that shut down my emotions. Better to not feel anything than to feel all that mess that was drug up from the bottom where I kept shoving it.

Mom was asleep in her chair. I quietly slipped back to my room and climbed into bed. I turned the radio on low. I was drifting off when a familiar song came on. My mind followed along with the melody, I knew this song. My sleepy thoughts roamed through the storage files in my head. It was from prom. My mind whisked me away to the dance. Everyone was having a good time; everything was just as it was that night. I was slow dancing with Nick; I breathed in smelling his cologne.

Things swirled and got darker.

My dreams of the void had always been in the meadow. I knew it would come, but this time it grew faster and bigger. Instead of me trying to stuff things in the void to fill it, it devoured things itself. The giant hole swirling inside me sucked things in, nothing and no one was getting away. Panic and fear rippled through the surrounding people. I ran for the exit to leave; I didn't want anyone else to suffer. It was out of control and I had no power to stop it.

Nick held onto my hand tightly. I tried in vain to get away from him. "You need to go, Nick!"

"I won't let go." He stood defiantly by my side. He didn't seem afraid of the swirling mass that was consuming me from the inside out.

I grabbed onto him with both hands. "You can help me?"

He pointed a finger to the far end of the room to where the spotlight was shining brightly on us. "No, but he can."

I shielded my eyes against the radiant light eagerly looking for the person who could help me. "Where is he? Why doesn't he come here?" I peered from side to side, trying every angle to see around the light.

"He'll call for you."

I had to strain to hear Nick, how was I going to hear someone from across the room? "What if I can't hear him?" I leaned forward, waiting intently for Nick's response.

"You won't hear him with your ears." He pointed to his chest. "You'll hear him here."

"What do you mean? I don't understand what you're saying." A new song blared through the speakers.

The void held steady as if it were waiting as well. I surveyed the room once more for this man who could rescue me. There were people who, like me, stood with a big swirling hole in their body. Some of them frantically ran around trying to fill the hole with things in the room while others stood waiting. A few had a person standing beside them, just as I had Nick.

"You'll know when you hear his voice." Nick assured me.

I shook my head, this was crazy. Maybe I was coming down with something and I just didn't realize it. I heard it, or maybe my imagination was just running wild. I read about suggestive thinking in school. You could get someone to believe they saw or heard something simply by giving them the idea and then providing a little reinforcement.

"Did you hear that?" I stared at Nick suspiciously.

He looked at me. "I didn't hear anything."

I heard it again. I focused on the sound, listening more closely. It was him; it had to be him. I turned. I had heard that voice before. Peace settled in my bones as I walked toward the spotlight. The void churned within. I ignored it. I was only interested in the one who could make it go away.

As I got closer, I realized it wasn't a spotlight; it was the man.

Light shone through him like the sun. He was the man from the meadow. The brilliant light concealed his face.

And then the dream was over.

Chapter 11

On Christmas morning Mom and I exchanged gifts. It felt so different this year. I sat thinking maybe it was just me. I was in a depressed slump, and the terrible thing was, I didn't really seem to mind it. I put on a happy face for Mom, so she wouldn't worry about me. It was a poor attempt, and I was sure she saw right through it.

Since the night we put the Christmas tree up, I couldn't get Nick out of my head. He was an ever-present thought, and I was constantly pushing the thoughts, memories, and feelings, aside. I regretted not going with Casey that night. It would have saved me from the emotions that kept welling up inside me like a geyser, but unlike Old Faithful, I couldn't put a time on when it would erupt, or where.

After Christmas lunch I headed to my room. I knew I should hang out with Mom, but I didn't want to endure her worried stares any longer. My phone vibrated on my bed. I didn't recognize the number. I figured somebody just pushed the wrong buttons on their phone and ended up getting me instead. Something compelled me to answer it.

"Hello?"

There was silence on the other end. They called me and now they didn't want to talk? The nerve! I tried again sounding a little irritated. "Hello!"

"Um, hi." The voice sounded like it belonged to a little girl.

"Yeah?" She's probably looking for Grandma so and so. I was ready to hang up the phone.

"Um, is this Emma?"

I racked my brain for voice recognition but came up empty.

"Is this Emma Parker?" The sweet little voice questioned

eagerly.

It piqued my interest; the phone number was from out of state. "Yeah, who are you?"

There was a giggle on the other end.

"Hello?" I wasn't in the mood to play phone, not that I had anything better to do with my time.

"Um," Another giggle. "I'm your little sister."

"Yeah right kid, I don't have any brothers or sisters."

"Yes, you..."

Commotion in the background cut her response short.

"I have to go now." she whispered.

"Who are you talking to?" The male voice demanded.

The blood in my veins ran cold.

"What are you doing on the phone?"

The man cleared his throat. "Hello?" He spoke into the phone.

I didn't answer, I couldn't answer.

"Is anyone there?"

The call ended.

Barely breathing, my icy cold fingers wrapped around my phone in a death grip.

It had been years since I had heard my Dad's voice.

I was trying to make sense of the whole phone conversation when Casey's text showed up on my phone. He wanted to know if we could hang out; his family was driving him nuts.

I okayed it with Mom, not mentioning the mysterious phone call I had received.

Casey picked me up, and we cruised around before ending up at the local movie theatre. We sat in the car a few minutes while Casey talked on the phone with his friend about which movie was the best.

A pickup truck pulled up to the door. The guy jumped out and waved at the door. Familiarity of the form and body language flooded my thoughts. It reminded me of Nick. I squinted to get a better view and then scolded myself for even caring. I grabbed his necklace and dropped it on the inside of my shirt. I continued staring in that direction, anyway. When he turned to get back in the truck, I got a clear view; it was him. Now my eyes glued themselves to the theatre door eager to see who he was with. I kept telling myself it didn't matter; we weren't together. The necklace reminded me of the words he spoke about his heart. I shook my head feeling like a fool. I wandered how many times he had used that same line, and I fell for it hook, line, and sinker.

A group of girls exited the building breaking my chain of thought. None of them looked familiar. The door was almost closed when it popped back open again. The girl that came out I recognized instantly. A dizzying flash of jealousy hit me broadside. I watched Andrea get into the truck smiling and laughing. More feelings rose, but I pushed them back down. Be strong, I told myself.

"Hey, hello?"

They drove away oblivious to my venomous stare.

"Emma!"

I turned my attention to Casey and offered a weak smile. "Sorry, what were you saying?"

He adjusted the heat and looked at me. "Everything ok? You've been acting weird since you got in the car. What's up?"

"Nothing, I'm fine."

He raised his eyebrows at me.

We sat in silence for a few moments.

"I had a weird call before you picked me up." I fidgeted with a thread on my jacket.

"From your ex?"

I shook my head. "No, it involved my Dad. I haven't seen him in a long time."

"Yeah, you've mentioned that before."

I stopped fidgeting with my jacket and stared at him. I hadn't told Casey anything about my background or my Dad.

He looked nervous. "You told me about it, there's like a hole in you or something because of him leaving."

I continued to watch him and remained silent.

He gripped the steering wheel. "Well, I think you were talking in your sleep when you told me."

Every nerve in my body went on high alert. "What else did I say in my sleep?" I asked innocently.

Now he looked like he was hiding something. Bits and pieces of the night in the parking lot filtered in.

I leaned over and smiled. "Still looking for a return on your investment?"

He sat for a moment, a smile forming on his lips. "Sure, if you're offering."

I cocked one eyebrow. "Still wanna take turns?" I ended my sentence without the warm, inviting smile I had before, in fact I was furious.

He seemed surprised by my action.

"Take me home." I sat back in his seat with my arms folded across my chest.

His laugh mimicked the one in the parking lot that night. "If you want me to take you home, it will cost you something, honey."

I couldn't believe my ears, what a snake! I stared at him.

"Oh, don't look so hurt. You actually think there is a guy out there who doesn't expect something in return for his time and effort? Come on, you need to grow up!"

I fought back tears of humiliation.

"Oh, now you're going to cry? Spare me the crocodile tears, it won't work!" He sat with a smug look on his face. "So, do you want a ride or are you walking?" His whole demeanor had changed.

I slammed the car door. It was getting dark, and the temperatures were dropping. I could have kicked myself for not wearing a coat.

Casey spun his tires as he took off, throwing slush over the lower part of my legs.

I looked at the theatre; at least it would be warm inside. There were a few familiar faces. I didn't have any money on me to see a movie and didn't want to explain what was going on in my life that ended me up with no ride. It was only a few miles home. I pulled up my hood and shoved my hands in my jacket pocket and walked. Within minutes big snowflakes fell from above. At least this time I knew where I was and what direction to go in.

As I walked, my brain had nothing better to do than to remind me of the day's events. They were all pessimistic thoughts. I felt like such a fool. I basically called Nick a liar about Casey being anything but nice. I had egg on my face for sure with this one.

The snow was really piling up now. My shoes were wet, and my toes were going numb. I had my cell phone, but who would I call? I had isolated myself away from everyone but Casey. I couldn't remember the last time I spoke with Stephanie. What kind of friend was I? Friendship works both ways I reminded myself. She could come to my house anytime she wanted, and she hadn't. I knew I was trying to come up with excuses to make myself feel better and it wasn't helping.

The sun retreated in the sky allowing darkness to reign. The snow was keeping people off the road apparently because I hadn't seen a single car. The city lights reflected off the snow making it light enough to see.

My head filled with thoughts of Nick. He told me if I ever needed him he would be there. I shook my head. No way was I calling him and then explain that Casey left me in the cold. His truck would be nice and warm though. Then I remembered who else might be in the truck with him. She must have gotten her way after all.

I took my time walking; I was in no hurry to get home. The later, the better; that way Mom would be in bed. The cold was numbing; it was nice, and it matched my mood. The quiet sound of the snow falling was peaceful.

I found myself on Nick's street. Since I was into self-torture tonight, I decided I would walk by his house to see if he was home; not that I would walk up and knock on the door. His parents would think I was crazy, and maybe I was. As I approached the house, I saw the truck sitting in the driveway. I couldn't help wondering if she was sitting inside laughing and joking with his family like I used to. The void grumbled, and my heart yearned. I pushed that feeling down to the pit of my stomach.

His bedroom light shone through the darkness, beckoning me. Was I willing to suffer the pain of seeing them together? I was already headed toward the back of the house. His room was at the end of the house and had two windows, one on each side of the corner of the house. The first window I came to was only a view of a boxing bag, or whatever it was. The bass in the music drowned out the words.

I unlatched the cold steel bar on the gate of the privacy fence and peeked around the corner to make sure no one was out back. Once I was sure the coast was clear, I stepped in front of the window. Nick wore a pair of sweats, boxing gloves and nothing else. He alternated between punches and kicks. He must have kept up his work out habits because his muscles were just as big as I remembered them. I took a few steps forward to get a closer look in his room to see if she there. My foot snagged on one of the shrub branches. I fell against the house with a thud. I spun around to run, but then thought better. I shrunk under the window hoping I was out of sight. A shadow fell upon the snow directly in front of me. After a moment or two it was gone.

I decided not to push my luck any further and took off around the side of the house I had come. I ran a little until my lungs felt like they were on fire from the freezing air. My breath came out in a heavy fog as I tried to gain control over my breathing.

The flashing Christmas lights added to the beauty of the snow that was still coming down. A hint of happiness passed through me. I hoped it would snow tomorrow so I could sit in the den, watch the fire, and drink hot cocoa; just like old times. Me, all by myself. Yeah, good old times, I thought sarcastically.

I let myself in quietly and changed into my warm jammies. I found the softest, warmest socks I had and pulled them on over my freezing toes. I sat on my bed rubbing them to get circulation back and warm them up. My phone vibrated beside me. It was Nick.

I ignored it. I continued trying to revive my frozen little piggies. I couldn't remember them ever being this cold.

My phone vibrated again, and again I ignored him. Pain tore through my heart at the thought of him being with someone else. I gritted my teeth trying to once again put this in the past. He was moving on and so must I. My phone vibrated a third time. I was feeling irritated; why was he even bothering me? He had sent a text this time. I would ignore it, but what if something was wrong, maybe with his sister or his parents? I picked up my phone and brought the text up on the screen.

'Its cold out here come to ur door pls.'

I walked to the front door arguing with myself the whole way. Why put myself through more of seeing him, knowing he had just been with Andrea. The void rumbled at me.

He had on the same sweat pants, his hooded sweatshirt now caked with snow.

"Can I come in?"

He was already in the foyer; what more did he want? I stepped aside to allow him to lead the way since he felt the need to go further into the house.

He pulled off his shoes and headed to the den. I followed wondering what brought him here.

The light from the foyer barely lit the den. He stood by the switch to the fireplace and paused with his hand ready to flip it. "May I?"

I shrugged. He was being too proper, something was up.

He bent down and extended his hands toward the flames. "Come here and warm your hands."

"Huh?" I tucked my hands under my crossed my arms and walked over to the fireplace. There wasn't a lot of heat, but it was nice.

"I know you were at my house."

I replaced the surprised look on my face. "No, I wasn't." I

stared at the yellow, orange flames lapping at the ceramic wood.

He studied me for a moment. "I would almost believe you except for one thing."

I didn't take my eyes from the flow of the fire. "Let me guess, I'm terrible at lying."

He chuckled. "Well, I would have almost believed you, but I have evidence you were outside my window."

I stared down at him. It couldn't be anything I dropped because I didn't have anything to drop. He was bluffing. I stayed focused on him as he rose to tower over me. He tucked hair behind my ear and smiled one of his lopsided smiles. If my heart had been frozen it would have instantly defrosted and melted from that smile.

"I followed your tracks in the snow." His hair was tussled from having his hood on. He looked like a mischievous little boy.

"How do you know they were mine? Maybe they belonged to someone else."

He raised his eyebrows at me, looking amused. "Well, the stride length, and the print itself was smaller suggesting a female or a young boy. There were no other tracks in the snow and the fact they led right up to your front porch." He looked confident. "I was wondering though, the tracks didn't come from your house, they came from the opposite direction. That leads me to the question of where were you that you had to walk in this crazy stuff?" He widened his stance and crossed his arms in protective mode.

My toes ached causing me to grimace. I bent down and rubbed them.

His laughter filled the den. "Ah yes, and the frozen toes coming back to life; classic give away that someone has been out in the cold way too long. Oh, and your cheeks and nose are still beet red." He brushed the back of his hand against my cheek. His hands were warm.

"Need I go on?" He seemed genuinely pleased with himself.

I gave him a look that told him if he said one more word

about it he'd be sorry.

He stood in front of the couch and patted the seat. "Come here."

I stayed where I was at.

"Come on. I'm not going to bite." He patted the couch again. More memories.

I sat down on the couch, leery of what lie ahead.

He sat Indian style at my feet and began briskly rubbing his palms together. He grabbed my right foot, promptly removed my sock, and held my toes between his warmed hands.

Pain shot through my toes into my foot. I winced and tried to pull away, but he held my foot tight.

"It hurts at first, just hang on." He reassured softly. He massaged my foot moving in downward motions toward my toes.

It felt amazing, and the pain subsided just as he said. He placed my foot on the floor and repeated the same sequence on my other foot. His hands were incredibly warm. I watched him as he rubbed and massaged; he did it with such love and compassion. A wave of shame smothered me. I had ignored him; I had been rude to him, and yet he still treated me with love. I jerked my foot out of his grasp and pulled it up underneath me.

A look of surprise flashed across his face. "Did I hurt you?" His hands were in the same position as if my foot were still there. "I didn't mean to."

I turned away and rubbed my forehead trying to stall to keep from having to answer.

He sat beside me on the couch. His hoodie swept across my toes.

"You're wet!" I screeched, pulling my feet away.

"Oh, sorry." He scooted to the edge of the couch and pulled his sweatshirt off over his head in one fluid motion, revealing his muscular back. He stood and glanced at the fire and then turned to face me. "Can I put this in the dryer or something?"

"Yeah, we have to be quiet and not wake Mom up." I rose to my feet.

"I know where the dryer is, I'll get it."

I watched him exit the room.

A few minutes later he returned to his place next to me. He stared at me for a moment and cocked his head.

"What?" I asked him suspiciously.

He reached over and put his hand on the top part of my chest, being careful not to touch where he shouldn't. His fingers traced the outline of his heart necklace. A boyish grin spread across his face.

I pushed his hand away.

"So, what were you doing out walking around in the snow?" He asked nonchalantly.

"What were you doing at the theatre with Andrea?" I fired back.

He frowned at me. "I wasn't at the theatre with Andrea."

"I saw you there; she got in the truck with you!" I interrupted promptly.

"All I did was give her a ride home." His eyes twinkled. "You're jealous."

"No, I'm not!" I retorted.

He bit his lip and nodded looking at the fire.

I watched him out of the corner of my eye. His chest was chiseled and perfect, his abs were awesome, his biceps as big as ever. I couldn't deny I was still attracted to him. Why was I subjecting myself to this? I stretched my legs out in front of me trying to push such thoughts out of my mind. We sat in silence for several minutes just watching the fire dance in the darkness.

"Why are you here? You want to know why I was out, or do you just want to punish me?"

He cocked a questioning eyebrow at me. "How am I punishing you?"

"You were right, Casey is a jerk! There, I said it. OKAY?" I crossed my arms and looked the other way. I didn't mean for the punishing part to come out, it was supposed to stay in my thoughts only.

He flung his arm on the back of the couch behind me and faced me. "Did he do something?" A fire burned in his eyes. He was still trying to be the protector. "I'm leaving tomorrow, but I will take care of it before I leave."

"No, he didn't do anything. I just remembered some things from that night in the parking lot. He proved that he's a jerk, so I got out of the car at the theatre and walked home."

His warm hand covered mine. "Why didn't you call me? I would have given you a ride."

"I thought you were with Andrea and I sure didn't want to be a third wheel." My heart ached.

He sighed. "I don't know what to do with you." He rubbed his thumb across the top of my hand. "How many times do I need to tell you?"

I didn't want to go in this direction. I jerked my hand away.

He grabbed my hand and put it against his chest. "Do you feel that?" The beating of his heart thumped against my fingers.

I longed to be held against it.

"It beats only for you. Not Andrea, not anyone else," He cupped my cheek. "Just you."

I stared into his eyes. I longed to get lost in them again; I longed to give in and to be drowned in his love again.

"Tell me you don't love me, and I'll leave right now." He whispered.

I swallowed hard. My throat ached with emotion. Everything in me screamed 'I love you!'; I just couldn't get the words to come out. Something inside overpowered everything else and refused to let the dam break completely. There were cracks and maybe even some leaks, but it held fast.

The room got hot. I felt sick. It had come down to this, and I wasn't ready. I didn't want to go there, but it was here, and I had to face it.

A tear slid down my cheek. I didn't deserve him. I didn't deserve his love or his kindness. I pulled the necklace out of my shirt and wrapped my hand around it squeezing it tightly. With one swift yank, I broke the chain. Another tear. "I'm sorry." I mumbled. I held my hand out waiting for him to take it.

He stared at my hand. The pain of rejection on his face was

almost more than I could bear.

His hands closed around mine. "I gave you my heart. It's yours to keep," His eyes penetrated the depths of my being. "Forever."

He cupped my face in his hands that now trembled and pressed his lips softly to mine.

Tears pooled in his eyes. "Goodbye, Em."

He paused only to slip his feet into his shoes.

I watched him walk out into the cold snow. I stared at the closed door unable to pry my eyes away.

I fought with myself all night. Sleep wouldn't come, couldn't come. Memories flooded my mind of our times together. He loved me, even though I was rude and ignored him, he still showed me love. He was fighting for our love and I was merely tossing it in the trash. What was so hard about admitting I needed him? That deep down I loved him more than anything else. How had I gotten so lost and caught up in everything else that the truth was buried?

Chapter 12

I stayed in my room all day. The cloud of depression was bearing down hard. I didn't eat or drink, thoughts of Nick leaving plagued my thoughts. I simply wanted to just disappear, like a cartoon character that shrank smaller and smaller, until nothing remained except a little 'poof' and then it was gone.

Mom called and apologized that she had to work a double, someone had called in sick and she had to cover.

As night fell, fear crept in. What if he showed up tonight? I decided I didn't care. I would push him, beg him if I had to, to put me out of my misery. I even unlocked the doors. I just wanted everything to end, to be over. As I looked back over everything the last few months, I realized I had pushed the feelings, emotions, and situations aside instead of dealing with them. What I thought was strength was nothing but a coverup. I had no strength; I merely suppressed feelings, and now they were all coming out. The dam was cracking, and chunks were falling, allowing emotion to break through in bursts. I had no idea what would happen when the dam crumbled. It was only a matter of time now.

I thought about the phone call I had received from the little girl. I picked up my phone half a dozen times intending to call Dad, but I chickened out every time. What was I so afraid of? I paced back and forth in my room. The more I paced, the more confidence I seemed to build. I picked up my phone and dialed the number I had stored under a question mark so if Mom ever went through my contacts she wouldn't know. Neither of us had any contact with the man who left us without so much as looking back. She didn't push child support because then he would push visitation or possibly even custody and neither of us wanted to be subjected to his angry outbursts anymore. It rang three times before I heard his voice.

"Hello?"

I opened my mouth and froze.

"Hello, is anyone there?"

I heard him sigh and knew it was now or never.

"Is this Jim? Jim Parker?"

"Yes." Came the response, "Who is this?"

I paused wishing I would have thought through the conversation topics before going off half cocked. "Emma."

"Emma?" He drew out the last part of my name waiting for me to give my last name.

He didn't remember me. I might as well just hang up now. "Never mind." I mumbled.

"My Emma?" He asked hesitantly. "But how did you get my home number? it's unlisted."

The little girl's voice echoed in the background.

"You did what? Why were you in my briefcase?" He sounded angry.

Memories came rushing back of when I was a little girl and his temper would burn out of control. I had to walk on eggshells around him, so I didn't set him off.

"Princess, why did you do that?"

"Do what?" I responded, caught up in the memory.

"No, Emma, not you. I wasn't talking to you." He barked.

"Oh, I guess someone has replaced me!" I balked. "I knew I shouldn't have called!" I hit the end button on my phone and tossed it onto my bed.

It rang immediately. I was sure it was Dad trying to call me back, and I wasn't going to answer. I paced again, chewing on my fingernail. Did I really think it would be any other way?

My room was quiet for a few seconds before my phone went off again. I ignored it. I remembered all the times he told me to be strong, and what was I doing? I was running away like a child. Maybe I should talk to him and show him what a good job he did raising me in my early years.

The phone rang once more. I snatched it off the bed and answered.

"What?" I hissed into the phone.

"It's been a long time, uh, Emma." He sounded distracted. Again, I was not a priority.

My patience already running low, I tapped my foot.

"I'm sure you have lots of questions for me." He laughed nervously. "I just wasn't expecting you to call so soon."

"It's been years! How is that so soon?" I scoffed.

"Yeah, about that." He cleared his throat.

"How did you even get my cell number?" I demanded.

"Well, sweetheart....."

"Now you want to call me endearing names like sweetheart? You haven't earned that right!" I sneered.

Did he think he could pick up where he left off years ago? I wondered if Mom had given him my number. When had she been in contact with him? I felt betrayed.

"I've meant to call you every birthday, every Christmas and other holidays, but I couldn't ever get up the nerve to do it."

I was stewing and did not respond.

He continued. "You know, you are very important to me."

I narrowed my eyes and clenched my jaw. Too bad he couldn't see the hateful look I was giving him over the phone.

"I do miss you, Princess. I want to say.." His voice broke. "I want to tell you..."

There was a pause. The emotion I heard over the phone only fueled the fire that grew in intensity with each passing moment he spoke.

"Can you hear me?" His voice sounded small and fragile.

"Well Dad, it's a funny thing. See, someone taught me you need to be strong, weak people don't survive in this world. You need to quit crying because if you don't, I will leave." My tone dripped with sarcasm.

"I was wrong when I told you that, Princess." He protested.

"Stop calling me that!" I shouted into the phone. "You are

nothing but a hypocrite, Dad! Buck up and be strong! There's no place in this world for weak people!"

A vision of his face twisted with anger from all those years ago surfaced in my memory. I ended the call and tossed my phone on the nightstand.

I tore the blankets off my bed and threw my hamper across the room scattering its contents as it went. I lugged my mattress off the box springs into the middle of the floor. I expected him to call back, and I would really let him have it. Anger spread through my body like venom. I stood in the middle of my mattress breathing heavily. My eyes darted around the room looking for something to demolish. I grabbed my lamp and launched it across the room shattering it against the wall. I had my clock in hand ready to tear it to pieces when my phone rang.

Here was my opportunity to really bring it home for him, leaving no doubt what I thought and felt about him. I really wasn't interested in what he had to say for himself or what excuse he wanted to conjure up.

"Ready for more good advice, Jim?" I seethed into the phone.

"Emma Renee!"

"Mom?" I stood clutching my clock; I temporarily put the thought of turning it into a projectile on hold.

"What have you done?"

"What do you mean?" I stalled, trying to cover. Did she know about my rampage?

"How could you be so rude to your father?"

That comment took me down a couple of notches. "How could I be so rude?" I huffed.

"He called me, and he's upset..."

"Good!" I interrupted loudly.

"No, Emma, not good. He asked me to talk to you."

Now she sounded mad.

"How can you just brush off what he did to us, Mom?" I gripped the phone tighter.

She sighed. "That was a long time ago, Emma."

I stood mouth agape and in shock. The one person I was sure

I could count on to be upset and mad with me about my father was Mom, and now she was bailing on me.

"We'll talk when I get home." She sounded drained, just like she used to when her and Dad would get done fighting.

I stared at my phone letting the rage inside build. I dropped my clock. I needed something bigger. I shoved my phone in my pocket and threw my cd player across the room. It crashed into my full-length mirror cracking it in half. The top part fell to the floor with a loud crash of breaking glass. The player bounced off to the side.

I sat on my box springs gasping for air as the anger drained away leaving behind a sense of despair. I suddenly felt so terribly lost in this big world. I pulled my knees up under my chin and hugged my legs.

Earlier this year everything seemed great, and now my life was in a downward spiral and I couldn't seem to pull out of it. Mom was mad, Dad was mad, Casey turned out to be a jerk, and I hadn't been in touch with Stephanie in at least a month. She hadn't even tried to contact me in the last couple of weeks. I had written Nick off because of my own flaws I preferred to push down in my gut rather than deal with. After the way I had treated him and ignored him, I couldn't blame him if he never spoke to me again.

Who did I have? No one, I realized sadly. I was alone. The void grumbled back at me.

My foot slipped off the edge of the box springs. I bent over and picked up the plastic baggie. I had forgotten to get rid of the pills. I rolled them around inside the bag with my fingers gazing at the different colors. If I knew what they were, maybe I could take one that would make me feel better. The thought occurred that I could just take them all. Would anyone miss me if the pills did me in? I was alone anyway. Their lives may even be better off without me causing trouble and misunderstandings.

The void inside pulsated; at least it would be gone, that big gaping hole I carried around inside me. I took the baggie with me to the kitchen, grabbed a bottle of water and walked back down the hall, debating with every step.

I sat on the mattress in the middle of my room that looked like a tornado ripped through it and stared at the pills. I poured them into my hand; they overflowed onto the mattress. The more I thought about things, the more it seemed that this was the only way out for me.

It took two handfuls and half the bottle of water before the pills disappeared down my throat.

I thought again about Nick and my heart hurt. I remembered he had left his hoodie behind. I retrieved it from the dryer and pulled it on over my head; I had to push the sleeves up a little because they were so long. I could smell him on the material. I buried my face in the fabric and breathed in deeply. I went to my dresser and took out his necklace I had broken and returned to my seated position on the mattress. I held it next to my heart. I mentally leafed through the memories we had shared.

He was one of those nice guys in life you rarely come across and he deserved better than anything I could ever give him. I had treated him terribly. He had been so kind the past month, and I was nothing but rude and hateful to him.

I picked up my phone and went back through my text messages that Nick had sent that I ignored and never read. I scanned through them feeling worse with each message I read. From his texts I learned that I was having a nightmare that night in the den. He was trying to get me to wake up. He relived that night with me, seeing my reactions, hearing my pleas and screams, and it killed him inside not being able to help me. He said he didn't blame me for my reaction to him. Through all the texts he assured me of his love for me, that I was special, and I was worth waiting for. The dam crumbled, emotion flowed, dragging me in the torrent that had been pent up far too long. The brutal attack in the park, the horrific assault by Des, the ordeal with Casey, feeling rejected by my father, and the worst by far was my denial that I still loved Nick; that I wanted and needed him desperately.

I dialed his number eager to hear his voice one last time. My heart pounded in my chest and my mouth was dry. I wasn't sure if it was the drugs or the renewed feeling I was letting live again for Nick.

"Emma?" His voice was groggy and deep.

I looked at the time on my phone, it was two o'clock in the morning. "I know you're at college and I know it's late but..."

"I'm not..." He interrupted.

"Please, just let me talk."

"Ok." He replied sleepily.

"First, I love how your voice is so deep when you first wake up." I sucked in a breath. "I'm gonna miss that."

"What do you mean?"

"Shh, I'm not done yet." I continued quietly. "I love your lop-sided smile, and the way you look like a mischievous little boy sometimes." Memories ran through my mind like a parade.

"Okay." He chuckled. "What's this all about?"

"I love the way you look at me when I get all embarrassed about sex stuff, even though I get mad about it." My face flamed up just thinking about it. "You have an amazingly hot body, but I am sure you already know that."

He laughed.

"I appreciate that even though I have treated you like a jerk, you have done nothing but love me." My voice broke. "I want to say I'm sorry, Nick."

"It's ok, Em," His voice was soft and caring. "You've been through a lot here lately."

"No, Nick; it's not ok!" Hot tears fell freely. Grief dominated my voice, "You've been extraordinarily nice to me and I have thrown you under the bus every chance I got. I wouldn't let you explain about that night in the den. I basically called you a liar about Casey, and you were right, he's a jerk!"

"We all make mistakes, Emma."

I closed my eyes imaging the thoughtful look that would accompany the softness of his voice. "Well, I'm over the limit on mine for sure then." I sniffed. "I hope you don't mind, I'm wearing your hoodie you left here. It smells like you." I smiled. "It makes me feel warm and safe."

"Good, wear it all you want."

I sniffed again. "Sorry, I'll try to get snot on it."

"Eh, it'll wash. I'll even come spray some of my cologne on it for you."

His chuckle put me at ease.

"You're too nice to me, Nick." I crawled over to my night-stand and took out the picture of the two of us together and stared at it. I wished I could go back to that time.

I sat back down on the mattress feeling a little dizzy; something was going on with my body. I didn't know what to expect from the pills, maybe nothing but getting me a little high.

"I'm sorry for causing you so much trouble." My speech was being influenced by the pills.

"Have you been drinking?" His tone was harsh.

I ignored his comment and stumbled on. "And I want to tell you that you were right... I do still love you, Nick."

"Are you ok, Em?"

I wasn't done talking yet. Just as quickly as the room spun, it stopped. I flopped backwards onto the mattress; it made my vision wavy for a moment.

"Too bad you're not here." I sighed.

"Just say the word and I will be."

He sounded fully awake now, and I felt a little bad for waking him up in the middle of the night.

"I just wanted to tell you those things before I'm gone. I wanted you to know the truth." My speaking ability was getting worse.

"What are you talking about? Where are you going?" He demanded.

"Do you still love me, Nick?" I giggled thinking back to all those butterfly feelings I had when we were first going out. I was experiencing that all over again.

"Of course, Em, always; now tell me what's going on."

I sighed. "I like hearing you tell me that, it makes me feel special." I scratched my head that felt like my whole scalp was crawling. "I'm gonna miss that too."

"Ok, Emma, what are you talking about? Where are you going?" His voice was stern with fear mixed in. "Emma, what did you do?"

I didn't want to tell him; I didn't want him to know the stupid thing I had done.

"Emma!"

"I took pills." I blurted out.

"What pills; where did you get them?" His voice reflected his worry.

"Some guy on the street... I was gonna throw 'em away, but I forgot." I was having difficulty concentrating now.

"What? When did you take them?" He sounded frantic.

"Hmm.. a little while ago." I held his necklace to my chest. My brain went on to the next thought that popped in my head. "I'm sorry I broke your necklace. I'm holding it next to my heart where you said you wanted it though." I sighed. "I wish I could see you one more time."

"Don't talk like that! You will be ok, I'm on my way." There was a commotion in the background. "Are you at home?"

"Yeah. Are you really gonna come see me?" I sounded like a little girl who had just been made a promise that was too good to be true.

"Sis, call 9-1-1 and send them to Emma's house! I think she overdosed on something!"

A female voice responded in the background, but I couldn't understand it.

"I don't know; do it NOW! I'm going over there!" Panic resonated in his voice.

"It's okay, Nick. That's why I called you. I wanted you to know I love you, and it's going to be okay." My speech was so slurred I almost couldn't understand myself. I tried to swallow, but my mouth was too dry. Where did I put that water? I tried to sit up and found I couldn't do that either.

"I'll be there in a few minutes, Em! Hang on!"

"How are you gonna be here in a few minutes?" My tongue

felt stuck to the roof of my mouth. "Aren't you at college?"

"No. I stayed home because of the weather." He sounded out of breath.

"What are you doing? You sound funny." I giggled as thoughts trickled in my brain of what he could do to make him sound like that.

"I'm running to your house, I'm almost there. Are you ok?"

I was having a little trouble breathing, I couldn't get any words to come out.

"Emma?"

I felt so tired. My heart beat violently in my chest. I watched the hoodie moving in unison with my rapid heartbeat.

"Emma?" He yelled into the phone, but I couldn't answer.

A loud crash came from the front of the house. I forgot to lock the door back, it wouldn't matter now if Des came or not. I watched the doorway, unable to do anything else.

Nick ran through the door and dropped to my side. "Em.." He caressed my face gently. "Em, can you hear me?" Tears filled his eyes.

I stared up at him. I didn't mean to upset him.

"I love you so much! Please, don't leave me!" He kissed my forehead. "Help is on the way, they should be here any minute."

I took in a ragged breath and closed my eyes for a moment. I struggled to get them back open again. It seemed so trivial, but I couldn't help myself. "Kiss me." I whispered.

"What?" He put his ear next to my lips.

"Will you kiss me one more time?" I struggled to make my voice louder.

He looked at me for a moment, fear in his eyes. His lips were cold from being outside.

"I'm sorry." I whispered. My breathing was still off.

"Shh.." He wiped tears from his face with a sweep of his arm.

"I love you, Nick." My eyelids threatened to close on me.

"I love you too, Em." His face contorted in pain.

My heart had been beating almost out of control, now it seemed it was struggling to beat at all. My arms and legs were too heavy for me to move.

He scooped me up into his arms and cradled me against his chest. His heart beat and the feel of the muscle under his shirt brought me peace. This is where I wanted to be forever; forever in his arms.

He was speaking out loud, but he wasn't talking to me. I listened closely, trying not to focus on the sound of my own heartbeat that was beating irregularly in my ears.

"Please, God… don't take her, not yet…"

The emotion in his voice brought sadness, but I had no tears to cry.

"Give her another chance, everyone deserves a second chance." His body shook as he cried out on my behalf.

"Emma, if you can hear me it's not too late. As long as you still have breath in your body, it's not too late!" His cool hands pressed against my face. "Can you hear me?"

I couldn't respond. My heart beat more loudly in my ears, thump-thump. My heart rate had slowed considerably.

"I know I should have told you this sooner, and I'm sorry I've failed you." He wept bitterly.

I wanted so badly to comfort him.

"God loves you, Emma. He gave his only Son to die on the cross for the sin of the world; for your sin and mine."

Wasn't there a Bible verse about that? I recalled memories of church when I was a little girl. We had memorized something similar. How did it go? 'For God so loved the world'… That sounded right. I searched my brain; it had to be there somewhere. I tried again. 'For God so loved the world, that he gave his only begotten Son.'

Thump-thump

Nick pressed forward. "We are all sinners, none of us are perfect. If you admit you're a sinner, ask forgiveness and believe that Jesus died on the cross and rose again; then you'll be saved."

My thoughts were stuck on that verse. I racked my brain knowing there was more. It popped into my head after Nick finished his sentence. 'That whosoever believeth in him shall not perish, but have everlasting life.'

Nick took in an uneven breath. "You may not survive this." Sobs shook his body, cutting off his voice. "But if you do what I've just said you will be alive in Christ, and I will see you again one day... Not on this earth... but in heaven." The last part of his statement was just a strained whisper.

Thump

I searched my heart for truth and found that I believed every word he had just spoken. I couldn't audibly confess, but I could still think it in my head. Would God accept that, would he be able to hear it? I had to give it a shot while I could still think clearly enough to do it.

Thump-thump

'God, I believe; and I'm sorry.' My heart agonized at the thought of how undeserving I was of any kindness, love, or mercy from God. 'I'm so sorry for all the things I've done wrong.'

Memories of me making fun of Nick for being a Christian floated through my mind. All the times I pushed him to be physical with me when I knew his stand on it. Thoughts came to mind of things I had done, some from years ago. I asked forgiveness for those things and things I couldn't remember.

'I'm sorry for taking those pills to end my life, it was stupid. I want to ask that you let me live, but I don't deserve the right to even ask.' I was sad thinking I may not see Nick again in this lifetime, but it was because of the choice I made, and I had to face the consequences of my actions.

Thump

There was another voice and movement in the room. Nick relinquished me back to the mattress. I was so tired. I just wanted to sleep for a few minutes. The sounds in the room faded. Sleep sounded so good. I was exhausted. I didn't have the energy to even take in another breath.

Thump

I found myself in the meadow. It was beautiful like always. The thick lush grass felt wonderful under my bare feet. Clumps of white flowers sprinkled over the meadow were stunning against the dark green foliage.

I walked along enjoying the warmth of the sun, soaking in as much as I could before it came. I searched for Nick everywhere, but I was all alone. The wind picked up, and I knew it was coming. Dark clouds slithered across the sky and the void inside me rumbled in response. Cold drops of rain fell, causing me to shiver.

The void appeared and whirled as it grew larger. There wasn't anything in the meadow I could use to attempt to fill the void. I wasn't sure what would happen this time.

Then I saw him; the man who shone like the sun. He topped the hill to the east and walked toward me.
I ran to meet him.

"Can you help me?" I asked worriedly. "Can you help me fill this hole?" I shielded my eyes trying to get even a glimpse of the man behind the dazzling light.

"I can." He replied.

Just the sound of his voice brought peace.

"Who are you?" I asked curiously.

"I AM."

My knees buckled beneath me. "I don't understand. Who are you?" The void became more violent within me.

"I AM." He responded again.

I stared clueless and only half listening; I had one thing on my mind. I could find out who he was later, but I needed help now. "Please, fill this gaping hole in me."

Without another word he stuck his hand into the void, followed by his arm, he continued until he was completely within the void, but the amazing thing was the void ceased to be there! I ran my hand over my stomach. It was just my stomach; no more churning, boiling void! Somehow, he filled the gaping hole inside me.

The dark clouds disappeared, and the wind ceased. The sun's rays beamed down once again. I was whole. I felt peace and an overwhelming sense of love, acceptance, forgiveness and belonging. It wrapped around me like a warm blanket on a cold winter night and comforted me in a way I could not express.

I knew that everything would be all right; no matter what consequence my choice to take those pills brought, He was within me and I would be just fine.

I wanted to wake up. I wanted to tell Nick it was ok, and not to be sad anymore.

Thump

I tried to wake myself up from this dream or whatever it was. I had a reason to live now; I didn't want to die. 'Please, God, give me a second chance! I want to live!' I cried out in my mind.

Thump - thump

I searched the room for Nick. He was to my left on his knees, eyes closed, tears streaming from under his lashes. The necklace he had given me hung over the top of his clenched fist. His lips were moving, but I couldn't hear the words. Two paramedics were now in the room with us. They forced a tube down my throat and called out numbers to one another.

Thump

"Her pressure is falling."

Thump

My anxiety level increased. How was I going to tell Nick I would be ok?

"I'm losing her!" The paramedic barked.

A man stood behind the paramedic on my right. He walked around my feet. He was tall. I couldn't see the features of his face, something blurred it. He never turned his face from me as he passed by the paramedic on my left and stood by Nick. He sparkled like someone had dusted him with glitter. The white linen he wore was dazzling. It had a pattern inlaid upon the garment. I couldn't make out the intricate detail; it seemed to change as he moved. The brightness of the fabric hurt my eyes, but I couldn't break my stare.

His presence calmed the anxiety inside that was scratching at the walls trying to get out. I was so wrapped up in him I forgot about everything else.

Nick didn't seem to notice when he took the necklace out

of his hand. He walked toward me, the necklace now dangling from his fingers.

"She's flat lining again."

I kept my eyes fixed on this man who was now bent over me. A glow surrounded him. Even though I couldn't see his face, somehow, I knew that he was beautiful inside and out.

I couldn't hear my heartbeat anymore. I was aware of the paramedics working on my lifeless body, yet somehow, I was still conscious. I tried to wrap my mind around how that was possible. Maybe the body was like an old TV set that once switched off still held enough juice for a few seconds before it totally went off.

The paramedic on my right shook his head. "She's not breathing, still no pulse. We're gonna have to call it; there's nothing more we can do." The paramedics stopped their efforts to resuscitate my limp body.

Nick hunched forward and flung his arms over his head in deep despair.

I wished he could see this beautiful angelic being… maybe he was an angel! Maybe he was my angel. He was still beside me. He placed the necklace around my neck. He touched the heart shape, the representation of Nick's heart, and placed it over my heart. The blur melted away and I could see the brightness of his face. It was the man from the meadow! His eyes were gentle and caring. As I looked deeper into his eyes, things became even clearer. I knew He loved me unconditionally, that He accepted me, but most of all, He forgave me, and I would be with Him forever.

A deep overpowering peace settled over me. I knew He would take care of Nick and help ease his pain. His lips never moved, but I could hear him. "I AM the way. I AM the truth." His voice surged with power. My flesh tingled with each word He spoke. "I AM the life." A jolt ran through my body like a bolt of lightning. It traveled from my chest to my toes and back again setting every muscle, every nerve on fire. My body arched as I sucked in a deep breath.

Thump-thump

Nick's head jerked up in response to my loud gasp for air. His eyes were bloodshot from tears and his face still torn with emotion.

Thump-thump

My heart beating again was such a wonderful sound; I was getting a second chance! I looked for the man, but he was nowhere to be seen.

Ignoring the confused paramedic who fumbled around trying to take my vitals, Nick leapt to my side.

My chest rose and fell with each precious breath I took. Breathing was easy again, not something I had to work at. I lifted one hand and placed it against Nick's hot cheek.

A smile spread slowly across his face.

I smiled back. "I love you." Emotion choked out any other words.

"I love you too." He whispered, kissing my palm.

"I will take care of your heart this time." I said lightly.

He looked down at his hands and then moved to the side searching the floor. "I've lost it!" He shook his jacket watching carefully to see if it fell onto the carpet.

"It's right here, silly." I held it tenderly in my hand for him to see.

He shot me a perplexed glance. "How did you get it?" He gently pulled on it. "The chain was broken, how did it get fixed?"

I raised an eyebrow at him. "You wouldn't believe me if I told you."

A boyish grin broke out on his face. "You were given back to me from the dead; I think I would believe just about anything right now."

I had to take a ride to the hospital. Even though they couldn't find overdose amounts of anything in my system, they insisted I stay a few hours for observation.

God had done a miraculous thing in my life, and I couldn't help telling every nurse and every doctor who stepped foot in my room during the few hours while I was there. Nick stayed by my side. He sat in a chair next to me with a smile plastered across his face that never faded.

Mom was totally freaked out. I knew I would get an ear full when we got home, but I didn't care. I had been given a new lease on life and I was going to take full advantage of my second chance.

When we got home, I listened to every word of the lecture with the utmost attention, and then I told her all the things that happened, including the man. Tears pooled in her eyes as she listened.

When I finished, she nodded her head. "Someone was watching over you." She rose to her feet and kissed the top of my head before she headed to the kitchen for hot cocoa.

Nick sat next to me with a stunned look on his face. "Wow."

"Thank you for praying for me." I swallowed hard. "I'm sorry for giving you a hard time about being a Christian." I stared at my knees feeling ashamed of the way I had acted and how I had treated him.

He chuckled. "Don't sweat it." He put his arm around my shoulders and pulled me close. "I'm just glad you're still here."

At one point in time I believed there was no way I could love Nick more, but this was a new kind of love, and it was more intense and selfless than I had ever known. We now shared a bond; we were both believers in Christ and our love for each other was magnified.

Mom returned and set the tray on the coffee table. She sunk to her knees with tears glistening on her cheeks. "I've been thinking about everything you've said." She wiped her cheeks and looked at us with guilt-stricken eyes. 'I want to believe too. What do I need to do?"

I turned to Nick for guidance. This was all new to me, and I didn't want to mess anything up. He happily led her in a prayer much like the one I had recited earlier.

The three of us sat in the in the firelight's soft glow drinking our hot chocolate in silence, marveling at the wonders of our creator and of His great mercy and grace.

Chapter 13

As I finished getting ready, the doorbell rang.

"I'll get it." Mom's voice echoed down the hallway. "Hi, come in."

"Good evening, Ms. Parker."

My heart thundered with excitement at the sound of his voice.

Nick and I had our differences in the past, more on my part than his. He was my first love and as far as it concerned me, he would be my only love. I grabbed my jacket and shut out the light leaving behind my room that had just received a fresh coat of paint. The color I chose was a blue hue that reminded me of the color of Nick's eyes. Cream and ivory colored pillows and curtains would accent the room.

Nick had helped me move my old bedroom furniture out in the garage, so we could repaint my room. I picked out a new bedroom suite; it was an early birthday present from Mom. I knew it was more for my sanity than an early gift. There were too many unwanted memories wrapped up in the old furniture in my room.

He stood in the foyer still shaking off the cold and talking to Mom about what events were in store for us.

I stood and watched him for a few moments, his gestures, his adorable smile, and his soft chuckle that always put me at ease. Snow speckled his jet-black hair.

He looked my way and raised an accusing eyebrow. "What are you up to?"

I couldn't help smiling as I walked up to him. "Who says I'm up to anything?"

Looking at me suspiciously, he narrowed his eyes. "I've seen that look before."

I raised an eyebrow back and smirked at him before slipping my jacket on and hugging Mom goodbye.

It was cold outside. The forecast promised dropping temperatures after midnight, hitting the below zero range. The wind would be a major factor in creating the freezing wind chill that could turn deadly if caught unprepared. Snow piled up along the edge of the road gave evidence that the snowplows had been by at least once this evening. His blade seemed to have somehow piled it higher across our driveway.

I was glad the truck was warm and took advantage of the warmth blowing through the vents. Nick made it out of our driveway with ease. It amazed me how he seemed to excel at everything. Though not as heavy as before, the snow was still falling. It reflected the street lights making it look more like early evening instead of night. Traffic was lighter than usual.

I wondered if the youth event at Nick's church would have diminished numbers because of worried parents not wanting to turn their kids loose on a night like this. The Youth Pastor almost cancelled but left it open for those that wanted to brave it. Nick considered that a challenge.

I was a little nervous. I had only been to Nick's church for my counseling sessions with Pastor Wayne in his office, except for the time I was running from the cop and stumbled into their youth building at the end of some service they were having. I was lucky I didn't get caught by the authorities that fateful night. I believed it was part of God's plan to get me on track with him. Not that God set the whole thing up. Being off track was from my poor decision making ability.

Finding that place in a part of town I was not familiar with, and a youth service going on a Friday night, was God trying to show me He loved me. I was happy to hand the reins of my life over to God. Before God came on the scene, I wanted a change in my life; but of my own choosing. Change took place, but the change that came I couldn't cope with. After trying to throw my life down the drain, I started counseling sessions at the church with Pastor Wayne.

I pushed the memories aside and listened to Nick humming along with the song resonating through the truck speakers. We were an item again and things were looking up for me now.

We pulled into the church parking lot already lined with several vehicles, and found a spot.

Jasper stood in front of the building motioning for us. As we headed toward Jasper, he disappeared around the outside corner instead of going inside. I glanced up at Nick to see if he sensed anything unusual.

He winked.

We passed the sidewalk and headed in the direction Jasper had taken. The snow was deeper here where the grass lay nestled under a foot and a half of snow. I was glad I had worn my winter boots.

I stopped cold in my tracks. "Ok, what's going on?"

Nick paused. "What do you mean?"

I gave him a cynical look.

"What?" He asked again. He turned and stood in front of me. He took my hands, which were cocooned in my warm black leather gloves. "Something wrong, Em?"

I loved it when he used the nickname he had given me. Staring into his eyes, I felt the warmth of his love for me. I gave him a mischievous smile.

Confusion danced in his eyes.

I batted my eyelashes at him. "You're so gullible."

His jaw muscle ticked once as a round of snowballs pelted his backside.

He smiled down at me. "Oh, you're gonna get yours!"

"Run, Emma! You're on our team!"

I peeked around Nick to see Jasper standing several feet away, one hand gripping a snowball with his arm cocked and ready to launch; his other hand motioning for me to join him.

I kissed Nick on the cheek and sprinted for one of two snow forts.

"I love you!" I called out over my shoulder.

"With a love like that, I'm glad you're not my enemy!" Nick shouted.

I watched from the safety of my fort as Nick raced to reach his. He weaved his way to his team, trying not to get hit as white powdered balls assaulted him from the sky.

We volleyed snowballs back and forth until someone mentioned Capture the Flag. The snowball fight came to an abrupt standstill. We went inside to warm up and go over the rules.

If you were female, you had to be tagged. If you were a guy and your opponent was a guy, you could tackle him in the snow or however you saw best to take him down. That brought out some manly grunts of approval from the small crowd.

I leaned over to Nick. "A guy thing?" I whispered.

He winked at me. "Of course!"

They used the area that had been divided for the snowball fight, and just extended the borders a little further. Teams would be the same since they were evenly split already on the boy to girl ratio. They gave both teams a few minutes to get a plan in place before heading outside to hide their team flag.

We sent out spies to find out where our opponent was hiding theirs. We had engineered a plan of pairs and solos that would tread across enemy lines and guard the home front. They paired me with Jasper and our mission involved enemy territory. We crept from tree to tree working our way across our space to get to the border. We tried to keep to the outlying areas.

Todd, one of our spies, was returning with vital information on where our rival's flag was and who was guarding it. The three of us made our way to the area where he had just been. Hoots of laughter and hollers rang out as team members ran into opposition. When we reached the garage, we concocted our plan. If the intelligence report had not changed, there was only one person guarding the flag.

I rounded the corner of the garage sneaking backwards. When I turned, I saw Nick ten yards away. I scanned the surrounding area looking for any sign of movement or someone waiting in the wings to tag me.

The pine trees that surrounded the area were like a thick wall of darkness. The snow was trampled all over, making it hard to see any one set of tracks. I walked around to his right, sizing up the situation. I hoped he would rotate in his position following me. He played right into my hands.

"Hi, Emma."

His back was to the garage now. I stopped and stared at him. "Hey, Nick."

"I suppose you are after my flag." He crossed his arms in a guarded stance.

"You know I am." I smiled and took a step forward. "What will it cost me?"

He kept his eyes on me as he spoke. "You know I can't let you have it."

"I know I can't have it silly, that's why I asked what it would cost." I moved forward another step. The snow was heavier now and the sound of it falling all around was so peaceful.

"You know if I tag you, you'll have to go our team's jail." He dropped his arms to his sides. "I would really hate for you to go to jail, Emma." A smile played around the corners of his mouth.

I kept my focus on him. Jasper and Todd moved in silently behind him, inching closer to our victory. I moved a couple of steps in his direction to keep his attention on me. "Can't we come to some kind of understanding?" I kept my voice sweet and threw in a little innocence to boot.

He crossed his arms again and looked at me smugly. "The understanding is you..." He paused. "And the two behind me will go to jail."

I stared at him unhinged at the jaw. How could he know?

Nick whistled through his teeth. Four of his teammates appeared out of their hiding places in the shadows created by the ominous trees. One stepped out just to my left; how I missed him before I didn't know.

Asserting his regal power, Nick pointed in my direction. "Leave her for me."

Todd and Jasper didn't stand a chance, but they still went for the flag. The four darted forward in a flash of color. They tackled and took their enemy to the ground before they were within five feet of the esteemed flag. Raised voices, garbled together with laughter, filled the cold night air.

After Todd and Jasper were hauled in the opposite direction, it was just me, Nick, and the flag. I had my eye on the prize and I would not give up so easily. I walked boldly up to Nick who was standing a good distance from his flag now. "You would really tag me? Couldn't you just let me get your flag? I'm sure one of your teammates would catch me, anyway."

Mischief glimmered in his eyes. "That would be treason, and yes, they would catch you."

I stood in disbelief. "Really; you wouldn't do it for the one you love, for me?"

"Nope."

"Then I guess you will have to tag me, Mr. Edwards, because I'm going for your flag."

My confidence poised, I moved to the left. He mirrored my movement. I took a few more steps to get around him, but he kept himself between me and the flag. He hadn't tagged me yet, so I still had hope.

I backed up a little; he followed. I took in the surroundings around me trying to formulate a plan. I backed up a few more steps, and again he followed. This might just work out to my advantage. I moved back further and to my left, watching the distance between Nick and the coveted flag grow. I faked to my right; he didn't flinch. I faked to my left, but he didn't buy that either. He watched me, amused at my antics.

There was a subtle movement to my right. Jasper had made it back already and was attempting another try at the flag.

"You sure you won't just give me your flag?"

"I'm sure. Do you know how much flack I would catch if I let you have the flag?" He raised his eyebrows questioningly.

I had no fear of him tagging me now. He would have already done it if he was going to. I got as close to him as I could without touching him. "Sorry about the whole snowball thing earlier."

I rubbed my hands together to generate heat for my fingers. "It was Jasper's idea to set you up."

He nodded his head. "I figured as much." He smiled and scratched his chin. "I know you would never be deceitful toward me, or try to trick me."

Jasper, donning a huge smile, grabbed the flag and threw both hands in the air in silent victory before stealthily disappearing out of sight.

Nick continued. "I know I can trust you completely."

I stared at the ground feeling terrible now. I tried to make myself feel better by telling myself it was just a game.

"What's wrong?" He chuckled. "You look like you just lost your best friend."

I sighed and shifted my weight from one foot to the other. I settled my eyes on the spot where his flag used to be.

Nick swiveled at the hip looking in the direction I indicated with my eyes. He turned back around beaming.

"Your flag?" I raised my eyebrows at him, waiting for him to catch on. It was only an orange piece of cloth that was found after rummaging through some storage closet, but it was their team flag; one he pledged to protect.

He continued to penetrate with his amazing eyes.

"It's gone..." I waited for an outcry from him about his precious flag being captured, but none came. "Do you understand what I'm saying?" Maybe the cold had frozen his brain.

"Uh-huh."

I was beyond confused. "What, you have another trap waiting to capture it back?"

He shook his head.

I frowned at him. If there was something I was supposed to catch on about, I had missed it.

He removed the gloves from his hands and put them in his coat pockets. His fingers were a welcomed warmth on my half numb cheeks. "If the flag was still here, I wouldn't be able to be alone with you. Everyone on my team will chase whoever stole it."

The longer I looked into his eyes, the more lost I became. When he was this close I had this thing about becoming oblivious to just about everything else but him.

"You look so beautiful." He rubbed his nose against mine. "I don't think I have ever kissed you in the falling snow."

I closed my eyes in anticipation. His lips were cold, but there was warmth there too. My heart beat faster in my chest. I didn't care about the cold anymore; I didn't care about the game, the only thing that mattered right now was Nick.

"PDA! PDA!" The voice shrieked like a siren.

Nick was backing away, but I wasn't ready to break off the kiss just yet. Kisses were few and far between these days and I didn't want to be short changed on this one.

He ended the kiss and smiled at me. "Ok, Evan." He called over his shoulder. His eyes still held me prisoner.

"They have captured the orange flag, team green wins!" Evan announced jubilantly with both arms raised over his head in triumph.

"Isn't he on your team; why is he so happy he lost?" I giggled at the lanky looking kid bunny hop back and forth a few feet away from us, kicking up snow as he went.

"Look Nick, I'm a bunny!" He shoved his two front teeth over his bottom lip.

"And a good one at that, buddy!" Nick assured him.

We walked over to the boy who continued to hop toward the youth building.

Nick kept his voice low as we followed behind. "Evan is kind of special. Physically he's seventeen, but not mentally. He's one of our challenged youth that attends church here."

Evan was trying to catch snowflakes on the tip of his tongue.

"He has a heart of gold. I don't think I've ever seen him in a bad mood. You can't help but smile when he's around."

"Why was he yelling PDA? Is that something he does a lot?" I whispered.

"Only when he sees it." Nick put his gloves back on as we walked.

"Sees what? Is he delusional too?" I was feeling sorry for this kid.

Nick's loud chuckle caught Evan's attention. He trotted back to us. "What's so funny Nick?" His green eyes sparkled inquisitively. A grin spread across his face as he waited for a response. The red pigment from the cold nearly drown out the freckles sprinkled across his nose and cheeks.

Nick gave me a sideways glance. "Can you tell Emma what PDA is?"

Evan avoided eye contact with me, and then without warning he turned and ran zigzagged toward one of the other students ahead.

Nick smiled as he watched Evan now jumping up and down excitedly about something. He moved a little closer, humor dancing in his eyes. "PDA stands for Public Display of Affection."

"Huh?" I wrinkled my brow at him.

"There is a rule for couples in the youth group at youth functions, no PDA. No kissing, putting arms around each other, holding hands, stuff like that."

"Oh." There was a rule I would need to remember; although lately, Nick and I wouldn't really have a problem with it.

Watching me intently he leaned down, his lips inches away from mine. "Well?"

Was this a test to see if I would follow the rules? There wasn't anyone left outside except us, and even if there were people I would have failed miserably, anyway. I liked his kisses too much; they were a weakness for me; he was a weakness for me. I leaned forward pressing my mouth against his. To my surprise, he didn't pull away. He remained where he was, allowing the kiss to continue. I was the instigator this time and if he was waiting for me to break it off, he would wait for a while. His soft, full lips made me want more. I pulled his body against mine. His arms wrapped around me in return. I knew we weren't going any farther than this, so I would enjoy the kiss.

His lips broke from mine and trailed down the side of my neck causing my body to tremble. I wasn't ready for the feelings inside that now rose like a tidal wave, ready to engulf me.

"Time to stop." He kissed me once more before straightening. Our heavy breath fogged up the crisp night air.

The reluctance in his voice made me feel a little better about having to stop.

Chapter 14

The night kicked off with food, fun and games.

Other than Jasper and Nick, I didn't know anyone. They were all very nice. I felt a sense of belonging, almost like family.

My thoughts took an abrupt turn to my Dad and a part of family I never knew existed until a couple of months ago. The new knowledge of having a little half-sister wasn't settling well with me. I tried to keep the feelings of rejection at bay. Anger edged its way in. He was the one who left. He was the one missing out, not me. I would shun him one day when he reached out to me, and I was sure one day he would. I wanted him to feel the pain and suffering I went through and was still going through. Visions of him driving off and leaving me crying enveloped me.

"Everything ok?"

"Yeah." I replied absent-mindedly, too wrapped up in self pity.

"Emma!"

Nick's voice shook me from my thoughts.

I stared back at him with a blank expression as I tried to pull myself back to present day.

He studied me for a moment. Whatever he wanted say he must have decided against it and stood in silence instead. We were surrounded with music, talking, laughter, and Evan acting like a monkey. Some were gathering by the stage for another game. The announcements blared over the speakers. I struggled to clear unwanted family thoughts from my past. I caught bits and pieces of the announcement. They needed two contestants, and they were pulling names out of a ball cap.

"Emma Parker." My name came across the loud speaker crystal clear. My head snapped in the stage's direction. "You'll be first contestant."

"Come on!" Nick grabbed my arm and rustled me through the bodies milling around the stage waiting to see if their name would be next.

Brother Dirk, the Youth Pastor, was pulling out the names. He was in his late twenties and from what I had seen tonight he was always pumped about Jesus and very animated in just about everything he did.

"The second contestant is...," He swirled his hand around inside the ball cap while holding his tongue just so outside his mouth and making funny faces. Those standing around laughed at his attempt at humor. He paused in his attempt for a name. "What?" He demanded playfully. "I'm concentrating hard up here. Oh, sure it looks easy!" He went back to digging in the ball cap and produced a name. "Jessica Finch!"

Heads turned in search of Jessica, but she was nowhere to be found. Someone near the back shouted out that her parents came and got her early.

"Ok, let's try again." Brother Dirk reached into the cap again. "Nick Edwards! You're the second contestant."

I peered up at Nick. He made the comment earlier that I would get mine, maybe this was my time. We were ushered up onto the stage and seated across from each other on padded folding chairs with a small wooden table between us. They sat a red button in front of each of us. The button was attached to a cord that ran into a small black box at the end of the table.

Bro Dirk had taken on the persona of a game show announcer and was going over fabulous prizes we would win if this were a true game show, but since it wasn't, he could only offer the winner a pack of chewing gum. He promised it was the best chewing gum available.

He directed his attention to Nick. "Considering you were a Bible Quiz champ I guess you know your way around this little system."

"Yes, I do." Nick responded proudly.

Bro Dirk explained that whoever hit the button first would

get to answer the question, and questions were worth varying points. He seemed preoccupied with doing something to the little black box. After a few moments he was satisfied and gave us his undivided attention. "Are you ready?"

I was sure I didn't stand a chance answering questions about the Bible against Nick. It had been a few months ago that I had asked God to forgive me and save me as I lay on my bedroom floor dying from a drug overdose; I felt a little ashamed that I didn't know a lot about his word yet.

Nick eyed me, smiling. "I'll take it easy on ya."

"Really?" I crossed my arms and stared back at him.

"Ready?" Brother Dirk glanced at both of us briefly before producing a set of little cards from his back jeans pocket. "Question number one, for five points." He called out. "What is your name?"

We both hit the button.

Bro Dirk looked down at the box. "Contestant number one; answer the question."

I cleared my throat before answering. "Emma."

"That is correct! Five points for Emma!" Brother Dirk announced overly enthusiastic. He asked easy, corny questions and each time I somehow beat out Nick.

Nick examined his button in between questions as if there was something wrong with it.

"Can't handle being beat by a girl?" I whispered.

He raised an eyebrow at me, a smile forming. "Round two is coming up. You're not that far ahead of me."

I winked at him. "I am right now."

I might stand a chance if these were the questions they would ask.

"Round Two! This round will be a little more difficult. Players ready?" Brother Dirk took a quick drink out of his water bottle and swished it around his mouth in a cartoon manner.

Nick and I eyed each other with our hands on the table, ready to attack the button.

"Question number one..." Brother Dirk paused. He glanced

at each of us before continuing. "How many books are in the Bible?"

I searched my brain and came up empty. Nick meanwhile, was hammering away at his button with no reaction from the little black box.

Brother Dirk watched Nick, a perplexed look on his face. "What's wrong?"

"Mine isn't working." Nick held up the button by the cord.

His facial expression made me laugh.

Brother Dirk seemed amused. "Hmm.." He scratched his head as he came and stood by Nick. "Let's see here." He grabbed the cord and followed it back to the box where the end was hooked to nothing but air. "Well, how do you suppose that happened?"

Nick grinned from ear to ear. "Oh, I am sure you know exactly how 'that' happened."

Brother Dirk walked back to Nick and placed a hand on his shoulder smiling at him. "Well, I figured with you being a Bible Quiz champ, your opponent here could use all the help she could get." He laughed as he gestured in my direction. "No offense to you, Emma."

I shook my head enjoying the joke.

"Ok, let's get this thing set up correctly." He went back behind the little black, suitcase looking apparatus and went to work.

"I knew something was up." Nick spoke across the table. "Me getting beat by a girl? Not gonna happen!" He crossed his arms, confidence fully in place.

"Ok, I think I've got it hooked up now." Bro Dirk nodded at Nick. "You want to give it a shot?"

Nick held an air of self-confidence as he mashed the button with his hand. A loud buzz sounded off. He tore his hand from the button and stood, knocking his chair over. He shook his hand and stared at Bro. Dirk with a look of disbelief.

The room erupted with laughter.

Bro Dirk shrugged his shoulders laughing. "I'm a Youth Pastor, not an electrician!" He motioned for Nick to join him. "Are you ok?" He stifled a grin.

Nick nodded his head while continuing to rub his hand.

"Just a little prank!" Bro Dirk slapped Nick on the back before returning to adjust the cords once more.

Nick settled back into his chair and stared at me.

"What?" I asked innocently.

"You set this up, didn't you?"

"I honestly had nothing to do with it." I smiled thinking how paranoid he was being.

"Uh-huh, sure."

I shrugged my shoulders at him; I couldn't help he was being weird.

Bro Dirk wiggled around some wires and then looked up at us. "Ok Nick, buzz in."

There was more laughter from the crowd.

Nick looked at the red button and then to Bro Dirk hesitant.

I giggled at him.

"Here, you try it then." Nick nudged the button in my direction.

I looked at him struggling to keep a straight face. "You're scared of a little button now?"

He narrowed his eyes at me.

"Come on, a big strong guy like you, afraid?" I teased.

That seemed to light a fire. I could see it burn in his eyes. He reached out and casually laid his big hand across the button. There was no shocking moment this time, only a light showing it registered.

The game got back under way and the questions were Biblically based. Some I knew, but I couldn't make it to the button before Nick. He was racking up points with the memory verses, at twenty points each it didn't take long for me to fall behind. He seemed to enjoy rattling off all that information. He slowed in his reaction time, obviously trying to give me a chance. The only problem was I had to know the answers before I could buzz in.

Bro Dirk took pity on me and asked if I would like help.

I nodded my head already knowing who I would pick. I had seen a picture at Nick's house of a small team of youngsters gathered around a trophy for a Bible Quiz Championship.

"Who would you like to help you?"

I looked out over the youth gathered in front of the stage. Some kids waved their hands at me, eager to join me on stage. I smiled politely and searched until I found the one I was looking for. He was talking to a couple of girls with his feet propped up on the back of the chair in front of him, seeming oblivious to the hunt for help. Nick was a Bible Quiz champ, but so was this guy.

"Jasper Owens."

"Jasper Owens!" Bro Dirk repeated over the loudspeakers.

Jasper looked surprised and immediately removed his feet from the chair, leaning forward he wiped off any dirt that may have been left behind. "Sorry." He called out.

"Can you come up on stage and help this young lady out?" Bro. Dirk gestured in my direction.

Jasper bounded up the stairs and took a seat beside me. "I might be a little rusty." He cracked his knuckles and eyed Nick. A smile forming on his lips.

"Just like old times." Nick held out his fist for a bump.

"Yep, get ready to get beaten!" Jasper bumped fists.

"Not gonna be easy to do."

They laughed, but it was clear there was real competitiveness between these two.

The questions went back and forth, Jasper was catching up, but he started with such a deficit of points I didn't know if it would be possible for him to pull it out. The youth were divided, some cheering for Nick, others cheering for Jasper. It amazed me at how much knowledge of the Bible there was between these two.

Bro Dirk had one question left. Jasper had really rallied from behind and now the game was now tied. I had to be the one to go against Nick, no help this time.

Nick was pumped from playing against Jasper and I knew I didn't stand a chance. Jasper had done a brilliant job getting me back in the game and I didn't want to waste his effort.

"This is for the whole enchilada, the whole ball of wax, all the beans.."

The crowd hollered out for Bro Dirk to get on with it.

"Ok, the final question of the game." A hush fell over the sanctuary. "How many of each animal did Moses put on the ark?"

Nick had the buzzer tagged before my hand even left the table.

"Contestant number two." Bro Dirk pointed to Nick.

"Two!" He laced his fingers behind his head, relaxing back into his folding chair.

"I'm sorry, that is incorrect."

"What?" Nick belted out.

Bro Dirk grinned at me. "Contestant number one has a chance to answer. Listen closely to the question. How many of each animal did Moses put on the ark?"

I waited a moment before answering. "None." I settled my eyes on Nick feeling my ego inflate as I spoke.

Nick shook his head, smiling.

"That is correct. It was Noah, not Moses. Contestant number one wins the game!" Bro Dirk said in his best announcer voice. "Here is the pack of the most excellent chewing gum I promised the winner." He handed me a small pack of gum. I stuffed it in my pocket, feeling triumphant.

Some youth gathered on the stage to congratulate me on my win. Through the crowd I caught sight of Nick and Jasper shaking hands. It appeared there were no hard feelings between the two.

Bro Dirk announced that it was still snowing outside, and we needed to shut it down early. We stayed behind and helped get things ready for services the next day. Rumors were already floating around that service would be canceled because of the snow. Maybe I would get lucky and school would be canceled too, so Nick and I could have more time together.

Bro Dirk shut the lights out and locked the doors. We stood in the parking lot talking for a few minutes before we each headed to our separate vehicles.

I was glad I had dressed in layers. It allowed me more freedom of movement, not having to wear a bulky coat, and yet I was warm at the same time. We sat in the truck as it warmed up.

With the winter weather Nick couldn't drive his corvette and had been borrowing his dad's truck. His parents found a four-wheel drive, king cab, truck. The price was right, so they bought it for him to travel back and forth to college during the winter months. It was a big, red, decked out truck; it had chrome bumpers, round chrome running boards and a roll bar with lights. It had all the accessories.

I reached into my pocket and pulled out the pack of gum. "Here this belongs to you." I held it out for Nick to take.

"You won; it belongs to you." He fidgeted with the vent controls on the dash. Pulling off one glove, he held his bare hand in front of the vent.

"Jasper told me." I confessed.

"Told you what?" He went back to fidgeting with the controls.

"That you knew better, that Moses had nothing to do with the ark." I waved the pack of gum at him.

"How would Jasper know if I knew better?" He avoided eye contact with me, confirming my suspicion.

"He said it was your favorite joke, catching people off guard." I held the package closer to him. "You are the true owner of this most excellent bubble gum." I tried to imitate Bro Dirk's announcer voice and failed miserably. I was hoping to at least get a laugh, but he ignored me and the gum, looking out the window instead. I gave up trying to get him to take the gum and stuck it back in my pocket. "Why didn't you answer it right; if you knew the answer?"

He turned and gave me his full attention. "I wanted you to win."

I watched Bro Dirk pull out of the parking lot, sliding as he drove away. "You don't care that you looked silly? That a Bible Quiz champ missed such an obvious, easy question?"

His features softened. "Not if it meant you would win."

I stared at him waiting for some smart remark.

He stared back at me solemnly.

"Awe, you're so sweet!" I leaned over and kissed his cheek.

He donned a boyish grin. "I know."

There was a hint of arrogance in his voice. I raised an eyebrow at him. "Full of ourselves, are we?"

"We?" He asked with mischief dancing in his eyes.

"Yeah, you and that mouse in your pocket!" I dug my fingers in his ribs. He looked at me curiously; then I remembered he wasn't ticklish.

"You wanna play that game, huh?" His smile widened as he intentionally removed his other glove, loosening the fit, finger by finger. He eyed me the whole time, reminding me of those creepy horror movies where the bad guy was just about to do something horrible.

"No, I'm good." I laughed uneasily. "No games here." I slowly scooted over by my door.

He jerked his body sideways at the same time I opened the door. I swung my knees to the side to exit the truck. I hurriedly put my left foot on the running board. I felt Nick's hand grab my jacket. I twisted around to get free. My foot slipped and somehow the tip of my boot got wedged between the running board and the truck itself. Our laughter rang out in the cold night air. I fell out of the truck. I landed with my stomach in the snow, my foot twisted and stuck above me. Pain shot through my ankle taking my breath away.

"You okay down there?" Nick laughed.

I rolled to my side, blinking back tears and stared up at him.

His demeanor changed instantly. He launched himself out of the truck and kneeled by my side.

Jasper jogged over, and he and Nick worked to get my boot dislodged as I whimpered in pain.

They quickly helped me to my feet. I touched my foot lightly to the ground and immediately pulled it up as pain radiated through it. Nick wiped the snow off my clothes while Jasper helped steady me. Hot tears filled my eyes. I was holding my composure for now, but I knew it wouldn't take much more to push me over the edge. I hated crying; it was for weak people and I refused to see myself as weak.

Nick finished brushing the snow off me, leaving wet spots behind. The cold was seeping through the layers and making my teeth chatter.

Nick stared at me with a forlorn look. "I'm so sorry."

"It's not your fault." I tried to hop to the truck on one foot.

Nick hoisted me up on the seat, visibly upset.

"I took first aid courses over the summer; you want me to look at it?" Jasper breathed into his cupped hands to warm them.

Nick moved to the side answering the question with a gesture.

"I'll try to be gentle, but this may hurt a little." He eyed me as he grabbed my boot; waiting for my permission to proceed.

I nodded slightly. I knew this would not be an easy feat because I always had to wiggle around a lot to get them on and off. Once I got past the ankle, it was fine; it was the ankle part that worried me.

He tugged gently once and paused looking up at me.

I closed my eyes and gritted my teeth, preparing myself for the pain that would be coming.

He wiggled my boot to loosen its hold on my foot.

I dug my nails into the seat. After a few moments I couldn't stand the searing pain any more. "Ok, ok, ok!" I cried out.

Jasper paused and raised his eyebrows at me.

"Just leave it, I'll be ok." Tears sprang to my eyes.

Nick paced back and forth.

"Emma, we need to get your boot off before your ankle swells more." He looked at me sympathetically. "I'm sorry." With a quick jerk, he popped the boot off.

"Ow!" I cried out in pain, my ankle throbbed more than before.

At the sound of my distress, Nick railed his fist into the side of his truck.

I turned and buried my face in the seat to hide the tears I could no longer hold back.

Jasper recommended I scoot back so my leg could rest on the seat. His cold fingers gently poked and prodded around my ankle. I bit down on my knuckle to keep from crying out again.

Nick's agitation was growing, and my crying out would only worsen his reaction.

"I don't think it's broke, but if it's not, it is definitely sprained pretty good." Jasper reported.

Nick flung snow off the hood of his truck with a swing of his arm and kicked the tire growling something under his breath.

"It's okay, Nick." I called out softly.

Jasper cocked his head sideways. "Either way, she's gonna need a trip to the ER."

Nick stared at the ground shaking his head.

Jasper tried to get me situated in the truck without causing me more pain. My foot felt better if it was propped up a little. Having short legs was paying off tonight. I could stretch my leg across the front seat and it wouldn't even be in the driver's way.

"It was an accident, nobody's fault." Jasper grabbed Nick's shoulder, rocking him back and forth. "Do you want me to drive you guys?"

"No, I got it." Nick shut my door and climbed into the driver's seat.

I called Mom and explained what happened and assured her I was okay. She would meet us at the hospital.
Nick and I rode in silence to the ER.

I wanted to assure him it wasn't his fault, but judging the mood he was in, now was not the time. I watched the muscle in his jaw tick. I would need to give him a little time to settle down.

When we pulled up under the ER awning a short time later, his mood had not improved. I opened my door and tried to figure out the best way to get down. The truck wasn't too high off the ground, but it was far enough considering my one-legged predicament. The slush waited on the cold concrete below, challenging anyone to trudge through it. I pictured myself hopping out on one leg, my leg sliding out from underneath me, and me busting my rear or worse.

Nick came around to my side. He ran his finger back and forth along the seat next to me. A look of guilt splashed across his face.

I touched his hand lightly. "It's not your fault. I'm clumsy by nature." I laughed softly hoping to lighten his mood.

"Let's go over your clumsiness." He tightened his hand into a fist. "There was your fractured finger,"

"I tripped over a duffle bag and fell." I reminded him.

He looked at me in disbelief. "Only because I scared you!" He cleared his throat. "The cut on your arm,"

"I broke a pitcher and raked my arm across it." I stated flatly.

He sighed loudly and continued. "Now your ankle."

I interrupted once again. "I opened the truck door to get out and my foot slipped and got twisted."

He furrowed his brows at me, shaking his head. "All of those things involved me. I think it's safe to say if it weren't for me, those things wouldn't have happened!" His jaw muscle was ticking again.

I smiled at him. "Still full of yourself."

His angry expression was exchanged for a look of confusion.

"I'm not letting you have ALL the credit, Mr. Edwards!"

He shook his head at me. "You're unbelievable!" He mumbled.

He scooped me up off the seat being careful not to bang my ankle and pulled me out of the truck, kicking the door shut behind us.

The wait in the ER was long and didn't help to improve Nick's mood.

The diagnosis was a severe sprain. When I hobbled awkwardly out into the waiting room on my crutches, I thought Nick would implode.

They canceled church services because of the inclement

weather. As the day went on it warmed up and the roads were clear by late afternoon, enabling Nick to head back to college to begin work on the campus he had volunteered for.

Before he left, I finally got him to believe it was not his tickle threat that landed me with a bum ankle. It was that or he was just tired of arguing with me about the subject.

Chapter 15

I slept well considering the throbbing in my ankle was less after the pain reliever I had taken.

The thought of cruising the halls on crutches at school didn't thrill me. I knew this was not uncharted territory I was about to tread upon and there had to be a way around it. I just needed to figure out my way.

The Doctor didn't want me to put any weight on my ankle and taking a shower in my shower tub was an experience. I was toweling off when I heard the doorbell. My mind went through a mental list of who it could be this early. I finished getting ready and bumped my way down the hall toward the living room where Mom's voice was coming from. I needed to get to school a little early, so whoever this visitor was would need to go away.

Jasper sat on the chair across from Mom and rose to his feet upon seeing me.

"What's wrong?" My heart raced at the thoughts that poured through my head like a sieve, leaving only the bad ones behind to dwell on.

"Nick asked if I could help you out for a while."

I silently let out the breath I was holding.

"I've already cleared it with Principal Slate to help you the next couple of weeks." He moved toward me. "So just tell me where your stuff is, and I'll grab it and we can go. I'm sure you probably want to be a little early."

I smiled knowing Nick had been thinking about me, and that Jasper was such a good friend to help me.

Every morning Jasper was out front bright and early. He escorted me from my front door to my chariot, which was his silver Honda sport coupe.

It was nice having someone help me with my books in between classes, and Jasper was fun to be around. He had a sense of humor and wasn't at all like all the remarks the others in school made about him; things like him preaching they were going to hell for their wicked ways. I had hung out with him for almost a week now and hadn't heard one word of preaching come from his lips.

It was becoming a habit to grab a drink at one of the local fast-food places each day after school and just hang out and do homework together.

It disappointed me that Nick would not make it home for the weekend. I wanted to spend time with him, but after speaking with him and the texts I received, it was apparent he needed more time to get over the whole idea of me being on crutches.

Starting out week number two on crutches was easier, but I wasn't a pro yet and I still needed help.

Monday was definitely a Monday. I got into an argument with a guy who called Jasper a Bible thumper. When I tried to take up for Jasper, the guy commented that I was just a wannabe. I opened my mouth to say more, but Jasper stopped me, he said it wasn't worth getting riled up; they were only words. He quoted the famous saying about sticks and stones.

I settled into the seat of the car the next morning ready to make Tuesday a much better day.

"I got a call from Nick last night." Jasper announced lightly as he backed out of the driveway. "He wanted to know how you were getting along. I told him you were doing great, and we were racing to class now." He chuckled. "I told him I had to give you a head start because you were whining about being on crutches."

I silently stared out the side window, my mind stuck on why he hadn't just called me himself.

Jasper elbowed my arm. "Funny, huh?"

I gave him a weak smile.

His amusement faded. "Yeah, Nick didn't think it was too funny either. He's still hung up on the whole incident and thinking it's his fault."

Caught up in my own thoughts, I went back to staring out the window.

Jasper explained that apparently Nick's phone had an accident and wasn't working; he was using a friend's phone. He asked Jasper to pass that information along and he would try to call sometime this week, but he was buried in essays and homework. Then more bad news, he wouldn't be home the next couple of weekends.

My heart ached at the thought of not seeing him for so long. He was a part of my life I depended upon for strength. Now knowing I would not get my weekend fix, I could already feel my world turning upside down.

It also meant he wouldn't be home for my birthday on Saturday. Emotion was brewing beneath the surface, looking for an outlet; any small crack would serve its purpose.

Jasper stared at me. "You okay?" He raised his eyebrows slightly. "You totally went from being happy to depressed."

I stared at the dash of the car. "It's not fair he can run away so easily." I whispered.

Jasper turned the volume down on the radio. "Sorry, I couldn't hear you. What?"

I shook my head. "Nothing." I smiled at him to cover my sadness.

He didn't look convinced, but he refrained from saying anything else.

To make matters worse, Mom informed that she had to work a double on Saturday, which meant I would totally be alone on my birthday. She tried to find someone to cover for her, but she was always the person to cover, which left no one else available. I did my best to convince her it was okay, we would celebrate it another day.

A dark cloud was settling over me. Its icy finger tips were

inching their way around into my brain stirring up unwanted memories and feelings. My counseling sessions with Pastor Wayne were over, but he told me I could call him anytime I needed. I had my phone in my hand ready to dial. I didn't want to give in to weakness; maybe I needed to give it one more day.

I slept in Saturday morning since nothing was going on, anyway.

Still no call or word from Nick. There was a time he told me he couldn't make it a week without me; he had just broken that record. I pushed thoughts out that tried to invade my mind.

My phone beeped. I jerked it up hoping beyond hope it was Nick. I was disappointed. The text, however, had good news. Stephanie had her baby this morning and everything was going great. Me and Steph were still friends, but our paths in life were going in different directions, and hanging out just wasn't as often anymore. The text also asked if I could come today and see them.

I racked my brain trying to think of how I could get there, short of hoofing it across town. The crutches really didn't make that an option. We still hadn't gotten me a car yet, Mom had the car at work all the time. I dialed the one person I depended upon the most the past couple of weeks.

"Hi, Jasper. Can you do me a big favor?"

When we got to the hospital most of the family had gone home after being up all night. Stephanie smiled at me when I poked my head inside the door. She looked tired, but happy. Daniel was crashed out in a chair next to the bed. I had gotten better at maneuvering around on my crutches.

"What happened to you?" She asked, bewildered.

I laughed quietly. "Long story."

She looked past me. "Where's Nick?"

"He couldn't come home this weekend." I stared at the floor knowing my facial expression would say more than I had.

Jasper walked in behind me. "Hi, Stephanie."

"Hey, Jasper." She shot me a questioning look.

"He gave me a ride." I blurted out.

Jasper scooted the other chair around next to Stephanie. After making sure I was comfortable, he put my crutches to the side.

Stephanie held out her little bundle for me to take. "We named her Danielle, after her daddy." She beamed.

I gently moved the blanket to the side exposing Danielle's plump, rosy red cheeks. She gave a little grunt and smacked her lips loudly, making us chuckle.

"She has an appetite like her daddy too." Stephanie touched Daniel's hand.

He sprang to his feet. "What?" He looked down at her blinking sleep away. "Do you need something, babe?"

She smiled. "No. Sorry, get some rest."

He rubbed his face briskly before noticing he had company.

"Hey, Emma."

He nodded his head. "Jasper."

Jasper stuck out his hand. "Congratulations, man."

A smile spread across Daniel's face as he shook his hand. "Thanks."

"She is so beautiful." I whispered. I studied her little hands and each little fingernail; she was perfect. She had dark hair like her daddy and her facial features so far looked like a mixture of both her parents.

Little Danielle smacked her lips more and gnawed her fist with toothless gums.

"I think she's getting hungry." I held her out for Stephanie to take.

"Speaking of hungry." Daniel looked at Jasper. "Are you hungry? I think the cafeteria is calling my name." He patted his stomach.

"I'm game." Jasper nodded.

Daniel leaned down and gently kissed his daughter's head before looking at Stephanie. "Do you want anything to eat?"

"No, but I think Danielle does." She laughed as the baby made her wants known a little more loudly.

"We'll be back in a little while." He kissed Stephanie. "I love you so much."

"I love you too." She replied softly.

I could almost feel the warmth of their love splashing over onto me; the desire to be near Nick stabbed at my heart nearly taking my breath away.

Jasper smiled at me. "You want something, Emma?"

I smiled back politely. "No, I'm ok. Thanks, though."

The guys exited the room discussing what food they hoped to find.

Stephanie stared at me through watery eyes. "I can't believe I even thought about having an abortion." She smoothed her baby's hair tenderly. "She was just born, and I can't imagine ever living without her."

We sat and visited until the guys came back to the room. By then Danielle had been fed, burped, changed and now lay asleep on her mother's chest.

It was just like old times, me and Steph. I didn't realize how much I missed her.

The guys stood by the door talking about hunting and following blood trails. How they got on that subject I had no idea, and I probably didn't want to know.

Stephanie gave me a strange look.

"What?" I asked.

A smile spread across her face. "You and Danielle share the same birthday. Happy Birthday, Emma. I'm so sorry I forgot!"

"It's okay." I said waving her off. "You've had a lot going on." I motioned to little Danielle.

"Did your mom bake her famous triple chocolate cake?" She asked, eagerly.

I shook my head. "No, she's working a double today."

"Oh. Do you want to hang out here? I mean I know it's a hospital, but I don't want you to be alone." She frowned.

"I'll be okay." I hugged her goodbye and then waited another 10 minutes for the guys to wrap up their hunting tales. Geez, and they thought we girls were bad.

I was glad I got home before dark. Since the assault by Des last fall, I was afraid to go into my darkened house alone. It made me angry that I felt that way. He stole more than just my innocence that night; he stole my peace of mind.

They still hadn't caught him. He was out there somewhere and some nights I could almost feel his eyes watching me. I shivered and forced the thoughts out of my head.

I fixed macaroni and cheese for dinner. I sat down in front of the steaming noodles. The doorbell rang. I turned the porch light on and looked through the peephole. It was Jasper.

I unlocked the door and opened it. "Something wrong?"

He smiled. "Yeah, actually there is." His green eyes reflected the humor in his voice.

I stared at him for a confused moment. If something was wrong, he wouldn't be smiling. I raised my eyebrows at him waiting for an explanation.

"What's wrong is..."

He pulled a small cake from behind his back. "You're spending your birthday alone." He reached down and grabbed bags of fast-food he had hidden to the side.

"What?" I asked, shocked.

"I didn't know what you'd want for sure, so I went to a couple of different places. I think I have something from just about every greasy place this town has to offer." He pushed his way past me and went to the kitchen.

I shut the door with a smile. Jasper was a good friend indeed.

Chapter 16

Before I knew it, another week had gone by. No call, no text, nothing from Nick. I kept pushing the thought out of my head that there must be someone else. Memories of us haunted me. I had no way to contact him. I considered calling Daniel, but I didn't want to involve him.

The company I had from Jasper was my only form of refuge. I didn't think about Nick so much when he was around, which meant the pain was more bearable.

At the doctor's office after school, they released from my crutches, but they told me to take it easy for another week. I realized with a heavy heart that without my crutches Jasper's help was no longer needed.

Even though it was just me and Mom the weekend went by quickly.

It surprised me to see Jasper at my door Monday morning. "What are you doing here?"

He smiled. "What do you mean? I'm picking you up for school."

"I don't have to use my crutches anymore." I held my arms away from my body as proof of the missing crutches.

"That's great!" He stood there for a moment as he realized my reasoning. "Ok. Well, if you don't want to ride with me, I'll go." He turned and bounded down the steps.

"Wait! I'll ride with you!" I cleared my throat to get the desperation out of my voice. "I mean, if you want me to." I tried to act casual. What if he decided against giving me a ride? Why should it matter so much? My thoughts were interrupted as he bound back up the stairs smiling.

"Sure; get your stuff."

I got my things together, and we were out the door. It was nice having a ride other than Mom.

We were going into week number three and Nick was still a no call, no show. I would have to face the fact that there was someone else, there was no other explanation. I cried myself to sleep several nights, my heart was breaking. If I could just talk to him if I could just.. I pushed those thoughts out of my head. It was time to face the truth, and the truth was Nick and I were over.

Mom commented more than once about me moping around. She kept a worried eye on me. I knew she was afraid I would try to commit suicide again. I reassured her I wouldn't ever do something like that ever again. I worked hard to hide my brokenness from her.

Friday when I got home Mom was waiting for me outside; her car parked on the street. Jasper pulled up behind hers and killed the engine. I watched Mom for a clue, the pleasant look on her face put any worries to rest.

"What's going on?" I questioned cautiously as I walked across the brown lawn that had patches of new green grass sprouting up.

Mom's smile widened. "Just a little something."

Jasper chuckled behind me.

I turned and narrowed my eyes at him. "Are you in on whatever this is?" I struggled to keep the grin I felt from breaking through.

He put his hands up in front of him and stepped back, trying to remove himself from suspicion.

A squeaky, grating sound filled the air. I knew that sound; it was the garage door. My heart pounded; was it Nick? I eagerly watched as the door continued moving. The vehicle inside was a newer model, red, economical, four-door I didn't recognize. I quickly searched the garage with my eyes looking for anyone inside. No one stepped out. Feeling my face drop, I quickly recovered. I didn't want to spoil Mom's fun, whatever it was.

She held up a set of keys. "Want to look at it?"

"Sure." I grabbed the keys and headed toward the garage. "You got a new car today?"

She walked beside me. "I didn't. It's yours!" She looked like she could not contain all that joy for long.

I stared at her. "What?" I replayed her words in my mind. "Really?" My voice sounded like she looked.

She nodded her head enthusiastically.

I sat in the car and looked around in awe, letting the words sink in. This is mine. This is MINE! It wasn't brand new, but it was nice.

Mom, full of excitement, stooped over with her head in the window pointing things out. Her excitement was rubbing off and causing mine to grow.

"Why don't you take it out for a spin?" She backed away.

I turned the key, and the engine purred like a kitten. I had heard the expression somewhere before and it seemed to fit even though I really didn't know what that meant. I slowly backed out into the street.

Jasper was leaning against his car, arms folded across his chest. His posture reminded me of Nick. A streak of pain shot through my heart. He waved casually as I pulled up next to him.

"Want to go with me?" I couldn't contain my excitement.

He looked pleased. "Sure." He got in and looked around the interior. "This is nice." He directed his attention at me. "So, where are you driving me?"

I shrugged. "Where would you like to go, master?"

"Master." He repeated the word slowly. He laughed and gave me a sideways glance. "I like that!"

"I bet you do." I replied, rolling my eyes at him.

I got behind an older-looking truck that had a bunch of junk crammed into the bed. After following him for a few blocks and dodging things that fell out, I decided on a different route.

We were a couple of blocks from home when I noticed my

steering wheel was pulling hard to the right. A few more feet and I realized why; I had a flat.

Jasper jumped out and examined the tire. He opened the trunk, got tools out, and rolled the spare tire to the front of the car. He grabbed the back of his collar and pulled his shirt off in one fluid movement.

Why were guys always so quick to be shirtless? Then I noticed the muscles in his back... and his forearms... and his biceps. I watched them flex and then relax as he worked at his task.

Brother Dirk's words replayed in my head. That night at the church he had preached about how we need to bounce our eyes. He explained the society we live in today had the tendency to show too much skin and we needed to learn to bounce our eyes to something else, so we would not be tempted. My eyes were bouncing all over the place, but they always ended up on Jasper.

In a few minutes he had the flat tire off and the good tire on. He wheeled the flat one to the back of the car and tossed it with ease into the trunk causing the whole car to shake.

We started home at a leisurely pace. He wiped the sweat from his forehead with his arm.

"Thanks for changing my tire." When I looked over at him, I noticed his chest and abs were just as muscular as his back and biceps. I wasn't aware of when he had gotten so buff. His chest muscles flexed, then relaxed, then flexed again. I glanced at his face to find him staring at me, fighting back a grin.

Embarrassed, I returned my attention back to the road again.

"Sure." He chuckled. He wiped his hands on his jeans before slipping his shirt back over his muscular physique.

I pulled into the garage and shut the car off still trying to recover from getting caught ogling the poor guy.

"You probably ran over a nail or something, should be easy to fix." He looked at me. "You like your car?"

I ran my hands around the steering wheel unable to contain my smile. "Yeah."

Jasper examined his knuckles.

My hands froze on the steering wheel. "Are you hurt?"

"Ah, I scraped my knuckles when the tire iron slipped. It's nothing big." He rested his hands on his thighs.

"Can I see?" I held my hand out.

"I'm okay." He insisted.

I continued to hold my hand out, waiting patiently.

He put his hand in mine for me to examine for myself.

I stared at his knuckles without really seeing them. I was too interested in the feeling that was going on inside my stomach.

I looked at him curious to see if he was feeling the same thing. He stared back at me with soft green eyes. I took in his features as though seeing them for the first time. His short brown hair was a little windblown from having the windows down, his face reddened and still sweaty from his workout.

I stared at his lips, wondering what they would feel like against mine. Without thinking, I leaned over. I caught myself halfway to his lips and quickly returned to my original position. I released his hand and stared at the bottom of the steering wheel.

Mom popped out of the door, saving me from my second awkward moment in the last ten minutes.

I needed to get a grip.

Chapter 17

I attended the same church as Nick and Jasper. I didn't feel like I stuck out like a sore thumb there, and everyone was nice.

They scheduled a Youth Rally at our church to kick off Spring Break. Youth from the same denomination around the area were all invited to attend.

As I entered the building, I felt excitement in the air. Students were everywhere, some faces I recognized, but most were new.

Once in the youth sanctuary I scanned my surroundings looking for one face in particular. My hopes were running on fumes, but somewhere I still held on to the thought Nick still cared and one of these weekends he would show up. I touched the heart necklace he gave me last year as a representation of his heart. I smiled as I remembered he told me I was the only one to ever hold his heart; that it was mine, forever. My search came full circle without seeing him. Another week had gone, with no contact from Nick. My smile faded as reality again set in.

Big hands came from behind and covered my eyes. "Guess who?"

I tried to untangle the sound of the voice from all the others that mingled in. I covered the hands with mine feeling their strength and warmth. My body tingled at the thought. "Nick?" My reaction was almost a squeal. I turned excitedly.

Jasper dropped his hands to his sides.

We both tried to recover from our apparent mutual disappointment.

"Hey, Jasper." I smiled at the genuine pleasure that surfaced when I spoke his name.

"Hi, Emma; glad you made it tonight." He avoided eye contact with me.

"Me too." I looked around the room at the chairs that were quickly filling up. "There is a lot of people here."

"Yep."

"Where are you sitting?" The thought crossed my mind he may not want me to sit with him after my blunder.

"I've gotta be on stage for worship, but after that I'll be on the front row on the right." He nodded in the direction he was talking about.

"Can I sit with you?"

A boyish grin broke out on his face. "Sure."

We made our way toward the stage.

It surprised me to see Jasper strapping on a guitar. I wandered what other interesting unknown facts there were to learn about him.

The first few rifts from his electric guitar rang out crisp and clear over the crowd. As the drums kicked in the crowd erupted into a bouncing frenzy. The excitement level rose with each chorus.

After several minutes the tempo slowed, and the bouncing transformed into a sway. I watched in awe as the worship team brought hundreds of people into the presence of Almighty God. Some had hands outstretched toward the ceiling, tears streaking down their cheeks; others stood in reverence. I focused my attention on the floor in front of me for a moment before closing my eyes and getting lost in the love that wrapped itself around me.

After the service, several stayed in the sanctuary talking and just goofing around. A couple of guys got on stage and played with the instruments. After a few minutes of pounding drums and guitars screaming, someone cut the sound while someone else cleared the stage.

That's when I heard it. Fear raked through my body with claws of steel. The sound terrified me. I wanted to run, but I was frozen in place. I tuned Jasper out, concentrating on where the sound was coming from. The hairs on the back of my neck stood on end as I realized the sound was coming from behind me.

Jasper put a hand on my shoulder that now trembled. "What's wrong, Emma?"

I stared at him, trying to get words to come out. My eyes watered at the unwanted memories that awakened. "It's him."

"Who?" Jasper searched the room.

"He's here." I whispered to myself. Questions filled my head, had he seen me, where was the nearest exit, and how long would it take for me to reach it?

Jasper shook his head at me. "I don't understand."

I finally found my voice. "One of the guys from the park!" I was afraid to move, it might draw his attention.

I could see the wheels turning in Jasper's head, but he wasn't making the connection fast enough.

"The attack in the park last summer? Me and Nick?" I reminded him. Nick almost died from that attack, how could he forget so easily?

Realization crossed his face, and he immediately scoped out the people in front of us.

"Behind me, he's behind me!" I spoke in a loud whisper afraid that my voice would be heard and recognized, giving away my location.

Jasper casually put his arm around me scanning over his right shoulder and then his left. I moved in closer to him, I wished there was a way I could climb into him and hide.

"What does he look like?" He asked in a hushed voice.

My brain quickly pulled up the vision of the attack in the park, causing me to shiver.

Jasper put both arms around me in a hug. "It's ok, Emma, you're safe." He was now facing the people behind me.

I swallowed hard. I wanted to believe him so badly, but he didn't know what I knew. This guy was vicious and uncaring. I couldn't fathom what he was doing in this place. "He's taller than me, but shorter than you. More on the heavy side, he has greasy looking dark hair, probably pulled back in a short ponytail, and he has a goatee."

Even though my verbal description was complete, my mental description rambled on, smells like he needs a shower, bad breath, cruel and heartless. His eyes are windowless like he has no soul. Snippets of that horrible day were prying their way into my head.

I had worked so hard with Pastor Wayne to get past this, to move on. Now it was staring me in the face, I couldn't seem to remember anything he told me to do to help get through it.

The raspy laugh sounded again. It seemed to echo off the walls, making me cringe.

Jasper picked up on it immediately.

"The guy laughing; it's him isn't it?" He demanded.

I nodded unable to speak.

His body stiffened as he moved me to the side. I turned and watched, unable to unglue myself from the floor, as he headed toward Rich like a torpedo locked onto its target.

"Jasper, no!" I covered my mouth to keep a whimper of fear from escaping.

Jasper's broad back blocked my view of Rich. His hands balled themselves into fists. "I think you and I need to have a talk right now!"

I had never heard or seen Jasper angry before. It stirred something deep inside.

"Hey man, what's going on?" Rich moved to the side with his hands held up in a submissive gesture.

Now that I could see him, I had to do a double take. He was dressed in a pair of khakis, a long sleeve button-up shirt, his hair was short and neatly kept, and he had lost the goatee.

I closed my eyes and listened with my ears, not believing what my eyes had just seen. It was him, no doubt about it. I opened my eyes just in time to see Jasper point in my direction.

Rich swung his eyes to where I was standing. There wasn't anything for me to hide behind; I was out in the open, vulnerable. He stared at me for a few seconds. His eyes seemed different somehow, but I was afraid to look deeper. I recalled the dark emptiness that was there before. I forced the memories from my mind. His demeanor seemed different from that dreadful day; this was not how I remembered him at all.

He hurried in my direction.

Panic gripped my heart. I bolted to my right, nearly knocking over Pastor Wayne in my attempt to flee.

Jasper had his hand on Rich's chest pushing him backward.

Rich had his hands up once again and had halted his advance.

"I'm sorry, Pastor Wayne." I locked my hands around his arm. I realized I was trying to force him in front of me, to get him between me and harm's way.

"What's going on, Emma?"

My eyes remained locked on Rich who was engaged in an intense discussion with Jasper, and now Brother Dirk who had shown up on the scene.

"It's him, Pastor Wayne. Rich from the park; he's here." Tears of fear spilled onto my cheeks.

He put his hand over mine. "Look at me." He said calmly.

I couldn't break my stare. If he came toward me I needed to get a head start even though I knew I couldn't outrun him.

"Emma, I need you to look at me." His voice urged.

I turned my head toward the sound of his voice, but my eyes remained on the cause of my distress.

"Emma, you are safe. He will not hurt you. No one will hurt you here." Pastor proclaimed.

I trusted him, and I knew in my heart that neither he, Jasper, or Brother Dirk would let any harm come to me, but panic and sheer fear refused to release its steely grip on my body and my mind. My face twitched with emotion, I fought to keep it at bay.

"You are safe." He repeated.

I nodded my head slowly, still unable to pry my eyes away.

"I will find out what is going on." He gently patted my hands and guided me over to a chair. "I'll be right back."

I reluctantly released his arm and watched him briskly walk to the small group.

I closed my eyes to get a hold of myself. The attack scene played out before me in flashes. Sounds of fists pounding against flesh, the smell of sweat, mingled with blood filled my nostrils. Mental pictures of Nick's beaten and bloody body. I shook my head to clear the vivid images that dug into my brain. My hands gripped the edges of the folding chair so hard it bit into my fingertips. I opened my eyes as fresh tears wet my cheeks.

Jasper and Pastor Wayne were walking toward me. I quickly wiped the wetness away.

Pastor Wayne spoke first. "He wants to speak with you."

"Uh-uh, no way!" I shook my head. "I can't!" I stared up at him, trembling. "I can't."

"I think you need to hear what he has to say,"

I protested again.

Pastor Wayne squatted down in front of me. "Emma, I wouldn't suggest it if I really didn't feel it would be beneficial for you. Here is an opportunity for you to ask questions you told me you felt you needed to know in order to help you deal with this." His facial features softened. "But if you really believe you can't handle it, you don't have to. I see you are very upset, and that's okay. It was a terrible ordeal you went through. You are in control this time, Emma. The decision is yours." He glanced up at Jasper and then back, reassuringly. "We are right here, and we will support you in whatever decision you make." He rose to a standing position.

I stared straight ahead and took in a deep breath trying to put my fears at ease. I wanted to know what he had to say. Whatever it was, at least I wasn't alone. I looked up at Jasper.

He held his hand out. "I'm right here. He won't hurt you, Emma. I won't even let him get close to you."

I took his hand and gave him a weak smile. "Thanks, Jasper."

He pulled me to my feet as Pastor Wayne motioned for Rich to join us.

My insides felt like gelatin on a plate being shaken by a child just for fun.

"That's far enough." Jasper commanded, slipping his arm around my shoulders.

Rich dipped his head once and stopped where he was a few

feet away.

I wrapped my arm around Jasper's waist pulling him closer, trying to find security to fall back on if my resolve wavered. Pastor Wayne stood just on the other side of us.

Rich stared at his feet a few seconds before beginning. "I want to start off by saying I am sorry."

His apology caught me off guard. I stared at him unblinking.

He lifted his head, eyes staring right at me.

I pulled myself a little closer to Jasper; in return he gave my shoulder a slight squeeze of reassurance.

"I wish I could rewind time, so I could erase those terrible things I did to you and that other guy." He pursed his lips together. "It was wrong."

One question screamed out in my head and carried itself to my mouth. "Why did you do it?" The boldness in my voice surprised me.

"We were strung out on drugs. You were simply at the wrong place, at the wrong time." He shook his head. "I know that sounds like a poor excuse, but it's the truth." His eyes watered. "Your boyfriend fighting back probably saved you both." He stared at the floor as if recalling memories. "With that group, it would have been so much worse if you would have begged." His eyes shot back to mine and held my stare. They reflected grief and remorse. They were no longer dark and soulless. "Did he…" He took in a deep breath. "Is he okay now?"

"Yes." I again fought to get the gory, bloody, pictures out of my head.

He nodded his head and crossed his arms. "I gave my heart to Jesus not too long ago." Tears streamed down his face. "I don't know how he can love a terrible person like me, but He does." He wiped his face with the sleeve of his shirt. "I got arrested a few months ago, for attempted burglary. I needed money to get more drugs." He cleared his throat. "My record was clean, but only because I never got caught before. I got probation and went to drug rehab. While I was in detox, a guy who worked there told me about Jesus." He shrugged his shoulders. "And I just knew I needed him." He directed his attention to Pastor Wayne. "I've asked Jesus for forgiveness, and in my heart," He tapped his chest twice with his fist. "I know He has forgiven me." He swung his head in my direction. "I ask for your forgiveness too."

"I don't think..." Jasper spoke.

Rich held up a hand to quiet him. "I know I don't deserve it, I understand that. I understand after all you went through because of me," He took in another deep breath and let it out. "That you don't owe me anything. I still ask for your forgiveness."

I stared at him trying to comprehend everything he was saying. Part of it seeped in. This was the same guy from the park, the one who inflicted so much pain and suffering on me and Nick. Could Jesus really transform someone so horrible?

Rich turned to walk away and quickly reversed his direction back toward us.

In desperation I wrapped both arms around Jasper and buried my face in his chest, my heart racing. I closed my eyes to hide from what might be coming. I felt Jasper's arms close around me protectively. I clenched wads of his shirt in my hands, hanging on tightly in case I was to be ripped away from him.

"Stop right there!" Jasper barked.

"Sorry. I didn't mean to.." Rich responded. "There's just one more thing I want to say."

I kept my arms encircled around Jasper and turned my head, so I could see Rich and still abide in my security.

He seemed undecided if he should proceed or not.

"What?" I asked softly.

"I know what Des did."

My facial muscles twisted as shame washed over me like a tsunami hitting me full force. It was bad enough that Des stole my innocence, but for everyone to know it, it was just too much. People knowing he touched me like that. I sucked in a breath, trying to keep my composure under control.

Rich continued, sounding like someone hit the fast-forward button on a recording. "He bragged about it to all of us after he did it. He's in the wind right now. No one has seen him or heard from him." Emotion plagued his voice. "If I wouldn't have lifted your wallet, he wouldn't have known where you lived. I'm sorry, I'm so sorry for what he did to you."

I fought to keep the sob from surfacing. My body shook violently as I tried to contain it.

"That's enough!" I felt Jasper's arms tighten around me.

Rich was saying more.

"That's enough!" Jasper roared. His heart was pounding in his chest, every muscle tensed.

"It's time for you to go now." Pastor Wayne stated firmly.

The movement I felt beside me I guessed was Pastor moving forward to escort Rich away.

I wanted to run away, to disappear. Tears flowed freely despite my eyes being clenched shut. Thoughts ran through my head unchecked. I wanted to be anywhere but here in this moment in time.

"It's okay, Emma. He's gone now." Jasper whispered. He gently rubbed my back to console me.

Sobs continued to consume my body against my will.

"Please Lord.." I whispered a prayer. By the time I got to the end of the prayer my sobs had ceased and there was a sweet peace. Terrible things had happened and I couldn't do anything to change them, but God still loved me and with His help I knew I would be okay. I released the fabric in my hands and patted Jasper gently on the back. "Thank you."

I realized Jasper was praying.

I remained motionless and listened to his prayer, my heart swelled with gratitude. Gratitude for a Creator who loves His creation, a Son who came and died for that creation so we would not have to be separated from Him, and gratitude for the good friend who was now praying for me in earnest. I listened to his heartfelt words letting them bring encouragement. A few minutes later he finished his prayer and gave me a squeeze before letting me go.

"Sorry." He mumbled wiping his eyes. He found a box of tissue and offered me one.

I bit my lip staring at the front of his now soggy shirt. He didn't mention it; although I was sure he felt the moisture.

He insisted he follow me home, and upon learning Mom was still at work, he did a walk through of the house to make sure no one was there.

We ended up talking about everything and nothing, just two good friends goofing around and having a good time. The later it got, the sillier we became. We then discussed sleep deprivation and the effects on the body, laughing most of the way through it. It was getting light outside. After looking at his watch he narrowed his eyes, and then they grew wider. That threw me into another fit of laughter. He decided it was time to head out.

I walked him to the door knowing I would miss him once he left. He could always make me smile and I needed that after last night.

He stepped down onto the porch to leave.

"Um, Jasper?" I stood in the doorway.

"Yeah?" He turned and took a step closer, looking at me sleepily.

He was still taller than me even with the step aiding me in my vertical shortcomings.

"Thanks for everything." I reached out and rubbed his shirt where my tears had finally dried. "Sorry about getting your shirt soggy." I teased. I crossed my arms to keep warm. It was springtime, but the early morning hours were still chilly.

"Anytime." He replied softly.

I didn't want him to leave, but I couldn't come up with a reason for him to stay. Would it be wrong to ask him to stay longer? I argued with myself.

"You okay?"

"I don't want you to leave." My hand flew to my mouth.

He smiled at me. "I don't want to go."

Slightly embarrassed at the sudden onset of open mouth insert foot disease, I dropped my hand and smiled back. Usually I was only so bold when I was sleep talking.

"So now what?" He asked sheepishly.

As I stared into his green eyes I felt butterflies take flight in my stomach. I leaned forward slowly, giving him the opportunity to back away in case I was the only one feeling this way.

He held his ground.

My lips brushed against his lightly before a twinge of unfaithfulness caused me to pull back. I stared at his chest trying to sort my feelings out.

"Something wrong?"

I sighed. "Nick."

"Did he finally call you?"

I shook my head. "I just feel like I'm cheating or something... he hasn't called, or text me, or anything, for over three weeks." Frustration broke through. "And I am the one feeling guilty! Does that even make sense?"

"It's okay, Emma. I understand." He turned to leave.

He made it to the sidewalk before I spoke up. "Wait!" I didn't understand why my heart was pounding at the thought of him leaving.

I walked to the top step on the porch and waited. The cold from the concrete seeped through my socks.

He walked to the bottom of the three steps and stood looking up at me.

"It's not ok, Jasper. It's not fair..."

"If you want me to, I can see if I can get in touch with him and tell him he needs to call you." He kept his eyes downcast. "I'll get a hold of him and let you know what I find out."

I bounced down two steps.

"You're a good guy. I know you're only trying to do what you think is right, but.." I cupped his face between my hands and shook my head. "I don't want you to."

"You don't want me to do the right thing, because it isn't fair for the good guy to lose out or..." His gaze dropped to my lips before returning to my eyes again. "You don't want me to call, because you like me?"

I let my action speak for itself. I wrapped my arms around his neck and pulled him closer. I closed my eyes once our lips made contact. No more feelings of unfaithfulness remained. I was getting lost in the moment; a feeling I thought only Nick could create.

After a few moments Jasper pulled away.

"Something wrong?" I asked with my arms still wrapped snugly around him.

He looked down at me and smiled. "No, but I really need to go."

"Just one more?" I asked shyly.

He fought back a smile, looking pleased. "Sure. You don't have to ask though."

This time he initiated the kiss.

Chapter 18

I finally gave up on Nick contacting me. As much as I wanted to be with him, I couldn't force it to be a mutual feeling. He would always be in my heart and strangely, I really held no ill feeling toward him.

Jasper and I hung out the rest of the weekend and all of spring break; we were almost inseparable. I thought it was odd we never went to his house; he didn't really talk about his parents either. I didn't question it. If we were together, I was happy wherever we were.

I took advantage of the no ask policy regarding kissing, but that would be off limits around the church. Although I didn't believe he had as much practice at it as Nick, he was a good kisser.

The weather was getting warmer with each passing day. I loved the green that was fast replacing the bleak colors and deadness that winter left behind. It was a perfect day for a walk in the city park. Jasper and I strolled hand in hand and fed some stale bread to the ducks down by the little pond. It was a different feeling being with Jasper, but it was nice.

It was late afternoon when we finally headed back to my house. Mom would be home at seven. I was cooking dinner for her since she had been working a lot of hours lately. There had been talk around the hospital about some new procedures and she may have to go out of town for classes. She assured me it would not be for a while and that she would not miss my graduation for any reason.

Jasper pulled up in the driveway making sure he gave Mom plenty of room to maneuver into the garage.

I got out and stood next to the car. I tilted my face upward, enjoying the warmth the sun was giving. A shadow moved over me blocking the rays. I opened one eye to find Jasper staring at me.

"What?" I asked opening my other eye.

He smiled. "Nothing."

"Uh-uh. Out with it." I demanded.

He stroked my cheek with his thumb. "I was just noticing how beautiful you are."

I playfully poked him in the stomach. "It took you this long to notice, huh?"

"No. I noticed a long time ago, but you had a boyfriend."

I dropped my eyes to his chest feeling a pang of sadness.

"I'm sorry, I shouldn't have said that." He rested his forehead against mine.

"It's okay." I attempted a small smile for him. "Are you always a good guy?"

He straightened. "Uh, yeah!" He responded without missing a beat. He winked at me. "It took you this long to notice, huh?"

I hooked my finger in his belt loop and pulled him closer. "Since you are such a good guy, will you do a lady a favor?"

He gave me a boyish grin. "Sure."

"Kiss me?"

"Yep." He lowered his lips to mine in a slow, drawn out kiss.

My heart was doing cartwheels in my chest.

Something ripped his lips away from mine. I blinked several times before I could get the whole picture situated in my head.

"I asked you to help my girlfriend out, not to help yourself to her!" Enraged, Nick threw a punch that jerked Jasper's head in the direction of his swing.

"You're the one who left her." Jasper spit to the side, leaving a spot of red on the driveway. He drew his hand across his mouth and wiped the bright, red, blood on his jeans. He slowly raised his fists. "You really want to do this?"

No, this couldn't be happening! I rubbed my eyes frantically, hoping the image would disappear.

"You're the one person I thought I could trust!" Nick yelled.

He plowed into Jasper ramming him into the garage door. The thunderous noise filled the air.

"Stop it!" I shouted.

My plea fell on deaf ears.

In the next instant they were on the concrete. Jasper came out on top. He fired two blows to Nick's face.

Nick fought back, and the two wrestled their way around the front of the car and into the grass.

"Guys! Stop!" I yelled again.

One minute they were standing and the next minute they were rolling around on the ground, each trying to get the upper hand. More fists flying. The sound of flesh hitting flesh rang in my ears. It brought back memories I didn't want to relive.

"Stop!" My pleas became more desperate. "Please, just stop!" Tears snaked their way down my cheeks. I couldn't take this. "Just stop! Stop!"

They broke apart with chests heaving to get oxygen. They continued to eye one another. I stared at them taking in the damage; both were bleeding and from the look in their eyes, they were ready to go another round.

I stood in between them to ensure no more swings would take place. I looked at Jasper first, then Nick. It tore me in two. I thought I had given up on Nick, but now he was here, my heart was aching again.

I turned my attention to Jasper and brushed my hand lightly against his cheek. "Are you okay?" I picked a few strands of grass out of his hair throwing them to the side. He continued looking past me at Nick with a scowl on his face.

"Fine." He said between clenched teeth.

I stepped directly in front of him wanting his full attention, but my height did not break the plane of his gaze.

I cleared my throat. "Down here, please."

He broke his death stare and settled his eyes on me. His countenance changed immediately.

"I'm sorry." He kissed my forehead. "I'm okay, Emma." He brushed his palms against his pant legs. He cupped my face in his hands and used his thumbs remove the wetness from my cheeks. "I didn't mean to upset you." He hugged me to his now sweaty body. "Everything ok now?"

I nodded my head and returned his embrace.

Nick cleared his throat reminding us he was still present. "Why don't you give me and Emma a few minutes alone?"

It was a demand, not a request.

"It'll be okay, Jasper." I whispered.

Jasper straightened but kept his arms around me. He took in the sight of his ripped shirt, "I'm gonna run to the house and change and then I'll be right back." He shot Nick a look as he emphasized the being right back part. "Walk me to the car?" He looked at me thoughtfully.

I nodded, and we walked arm in arm toward his car.

He stood a few moments with the door open. "I can stay if you want me to."

I looked over at Nick who was standing in the yard with his arms crossed watching us. "I'll be okay."

"You sure?"

I didn't know if he was being a good guy or if he was fishing for an invitation to stay.

"I won't be gone long." He started to get in his car and paused.

I raised my eyebrows at him questioningly.

"I believe our kiss was interrupted earlier." His eyes dropped to my lips. "May I?"

I smiled at him. "Yep."

He brushed his lips against mine lightly.

"Is your lip sore?"

He frowned. "No, why?"

"Because that kiss was seriously lacking. Now if you were wounded, I could let it slide…" I bit my lip to keep from smiling.

"Hmm." He wiped sweat off his brow with his arm. "Well, what's the punishment?" He played along.

I shook my head staring at the ground like it would be dreadful. I glanced back up at him.

He raised his eyebrows at me.

"Guess you'll have to do it again, and again, until you can get it right." I pursed my lips together. "I know it's gonna be tough, but you'll just have to buck up and take it like a man."

He grinned. "I think I can do that." He leaned down and kissed me a little differently and paused, his lips only inches from mine. "Better?"

"A little." I encouraged.

After the next kiss, he paused. "Better yet?"

"I think it's getting there." I giggled.

He pulled me close to him. "It's a work in progress. This might take a while. I need the practice."

Another kiss drown out my giggle. This kiss was the one. It reminded me of what the woman in the old movies must have felt when the man kissed her and her foot looked like it was hooked to a spring at her knee and it would kick out behind her. When the kiss ended, it took me a moment to get my bearings.

Jasper chuckled softly. "Guess that one passed on your scale."

I sighed, which only made him laugh again.

He turned his head toward the yard. "If you need me, call."

I had forgotten Nick was standing there.

"I'm sure I'll be fine." I felt my cheeks redden.

He got in his car and drove away.

I invited Nick into the house, not sure how to pursue conversation after what just took place with Jasper. I grabbed two bottles of water from the kitchen and sat in the den. Not wanting to be mistaken that there was a certain place he was to sit, I left his on the outside edge of the coffee table. Memories came rushing back. I stared at the bottle in my hand afraid to look anywhere else that might trigger another memory.

He snatched the bottle and downed half before replacing the lid.

The silence was awkward. I stole a glance at him. He looked like he was still boiling.

"He just had to kiss you before he left. Kind of rubbing it in; is that it?" His voice was low and filled with anger.

"He asked if he could kiss me." I replied in disbelief. I stood and walked to the bathroom and wet down a washcloth.

Nick was hot on my heels.

"Oh, well if he asked, I guess that's ok." He sounded off sarcastically. His grip tightened on the bottle in his hand causing the plastic to pop.

"Why do you care?" I asked snidely as I walked past him back toward the den.

"Why do I care?" He turned with a shocked look and followed. "Really? I can't believe you even have to ask." He stood in the doorway of the den and ran his fingers through his perfect hair. "I come home to find another guy kissing my girl!" He flared his arms out. "What am I supposed to do?"

I threw the wet washcloth at him. "Here! Your face is bleeding from doing what you thought you should do!" I watched as he wiped the sweat, blood and dirt off his face and shook my head allowing the anger to seep in.

"What are you supposed to do, Nick?" I raised my voice. "I'll tell you what you are supposed to do! You're supposed to call, or text, or write... Anything Nick, something! For weeks I didn't hear from you." Emotion brewed deep in the pit of my stomach. "You ignored me! You pushed me off to the side..." I covered my eyes for a moment. Pain and anger mixed, confusing my thoughts. "Was I supposed to just assume we were still together? Was I supposed to just wait until you were done hiding, or feeling sorry for yourself, or whatever you were doing?" I walked over to the darkened fireplace and stared at the cold, gray ceramic wood.

"I didn't know you would be so quick to pick up the first guy who came along." He scoffed.

I whirled around and stormed toward him. "This is not my fault!" I stuck my finger in his chest. "It's yours! If you would have just told me something, Nick!" Tears were building and for once I didn't care. My voice dropped to a whisper as pain won out over anger. "If you would have asked, I would have waited for you forever." I stared at the floor letting the tears rain down on the carpet.

I jerked away when he touched my shoulder. He touched me again. I moved away. I didn't want his pity, or his sympathy.

He wrapped his arms around me, and drew me to him. I pushed against his chest knowing I would not get anywhere, but at least he would get the hint. My frustration level was growing along with old desires of him being so near; his cologne, the smell of his skin. It wasn't fair.

"Stop." His voice was gruff.

I continued to push as tears plummeted down my cheeks. I wanted to be mad at him, but old feelings resurfacing made it very difficult.

His arms tightened around me even more. He spoke softly. "Please, stop."

I stared at his chest unable to move now.

He loosened his hold. "I felt like it was always my fault you were getting hurt." He shook his head. "When I saw you on crutches because of me…" He clenched his jaw.

"They were all accidents, Nick, nobody's fault." I whispered.

He relaxed his arms a little more. "I'm sorry I made things complicated, I didn't mean to."

I continued to stare at his chest afraid to look him in the face. "If I had any inclination, if you would have given me any idea that," I took in a ragged breath trying to keep emotions in check. "That you still loved me, I would have never let myself feel anything for Jasper." My insides were tied in knots. "I thought you found someone else." My voice shook with an emotion that was threatening to break down my stronghold, which at this point wasn't strong at all.

He pressed his lips against my forehead. "There isn't anyone else for me, just you." He pulled me back to him and rested his chin on the top of my head.

I felt guilty for enjoying his embrace.

He smoothed my hair and sighed. "I'm sorry. You're right, I should have called or something." He ran his hand across the back of my neck. His fingers found the chain and a gentle tug revealed the heart-shaped diamond necklace he had given me. He looked down at me, a smile forming on his lips.

"You're wearing it." His face lit up like a little boy who just realized the largest gift under the Christmas tree had his name on it. "My heart is yours…" He paused. "If you still want it." His eyes searched mine.

I had missed the intensity of his gaze.

He leaned forward.

I knew what was next. I couldn't help myself, I wanted it; I felt like I needed it desperately. My heart went wild in my chest at the thought of it.

The kiss made me melt inside. I wrapped my arms around him pulling him closer. I was getting lost in the feelings that draped over me like a blanket.

I heard the door in the foyer and quickly pulled away remembering that Jasper would come back. I glanced out the bay window in the front room as I walked to the front door.

Jasper was already getting into his car. I stood in the front room watching as he drove away.

Did he hear our conversation and assume by my actions what my decision was? I felt terrible, I could only imagine how he must be feeling. Everything was so messed up now.

I sighed.

Nick stood close behind me. "Do you want me to leave?"

I continued to stare out the window, feelings of remorse stirring in my heart. "I don't know what I want anymore."

Nick stayed longer. It felt awkward being around him again, but it was part of a routine I dearly missed.

I was glad I had dinner preparations to occupy our time. It was a simple box dinner, but I drug it out as much as possible. I was hoping it appeared I was concentrating on cooking and not avoiding him. I was thankful he left before Mom got home. It would be easier not to have to explain anything, especially since I wasn't sure what was going on.

After dinner I went to my room trying to make sense of what happened.

I called Pastor Wayne, and he agreed to meet me even though it was late. His wife came along with him and sat in the receptionist area outside his office looking in every so often through the blinds. There was a legality thing we needed to have a third party there. I sat in the leather chair next to the little table by the window. Pastor Wayne sat in his usual chair when we did our counseling sessions before. His office felt nice and cozy, which put me more at ease.

"What's on your mind, Emma?" He interlaced his fingers in his lap.

Pastor Wayne was a kind looking, soft-spoken man. He seemed to genuinely care and for some odd reason I felt like I could tell him anything.

I thought for a moment. "Is it possible to love two people at the same time?"

He eyed me before he spoke. "I assume you're not speaking of love such as for a sibling or parent." He crossed his legs. "Why don't you give me a little more information?"

"Well, I was going out with Nick Edwards."

He nodded his head.

"After I hurt my ankle that night at the church, he blamed himself, and when he went back to college he didn't call or text or anything." I started fidgeted with the sleeve of my jacket. "I thought he found somebody else."

"Did he?"

I paused in my fidgeting. "No, but there's more to tell first."

"Ok."

"Jasper Owens helped me at school since I was on crutches, and we hung out and did homework together." I smiled remembering the last few weeks.

"You like Jasper?"

I couldn't deny it to myself or to him. "Yeah." I smiled.

He waited for me to continue.

"Ok, long story short." I scooted to the edge of my chair and stared at my knees. "Jasper and I were kissing, Nick showed up out of nowhere and they ended up getting in a fight." I looked up at him to see if I would be in trouble for kissing a boy.

"Yes, I saw Jasper after the fight."

"Oh." I wandered if he told Pastor Wayne about me kissing Nick too. I continued with my quest. "I just don't understand." I propped my elbows on my knees and rested my head in my hands. "I still have feelings for Nick, but I have feelings for Jasper too. I feel like I'm being ripped in half. If I choose Nick, it isn't fair to Jasper, and if I choose Jasper, it isn't fair to Nick because he didn't ever really break up with me." Frustration was building again.

"You and Nick went through some traumatic events together, didn't you?"

Thoughts of the attack at the park and the assault by Des ran through my mind. I nodded.

"That can create a very strong bond between two people." He cleared his throat. "Jasper was there to help you when you needed it too. Is it possible he was just a fill in for Nick while Nick wasn't around?"

I stared at him trying to sort through my thoughts.
"I don't think so. I didn't like Jasper until after I thought Nick and I were through." I ran my hands through my hair and slumped back in the chair. "I don't know." I whined. I closed my eyes. "I know I don't want to hurt anyone, but I can't see a way around it."

"Think for a moment before you answer." He waited until I opened my eyes and focused on him. "Have you already decided in your heart?"

I searched my feelings, hoping for truth that must be hidden somewhere deep inside. After what seemed like an eternity I shook my head. "I don't know."

"It is possible you love them both, in different ways, for different reasons."

I sighed and looked at him shaking my head. "What does that mean?"

"You must decide between the two."

I scratched my head, feeling irritated. I knew that much already.

"I want you to know that I am being unbiased, and everything you have told me is in strict confidence." He gave me a compassionate look. "I can't tell you who to choose. You will have to do some soul searching and pay attention to your feelings and why you feel that way." He uncrossed his legs.

"Isn't there a simpler solution?" I asked, shifting to an upright position in my chair.

He smiled at me sympathetically. "I'm afraid not, Emma."

"Thanks for the advice." I said politely although I didn't feel like he had really helped me any.

He moved to the edge of his seat. "I would like to pray with you before you leave. Is that all right?"

I nodded and bowed my head.

I tried calling Jasper on my way home from the church, but he didn't pick up. Once I was home, I tried calling several more times. His phone kept going to voice mail. I felt I had betrayed him. I needed to talk to him and explain my side of things.

Worse still, was that I didn't know how he felt. We hadn't expressed feelings for each other verbally; instead it was implied by physical aspects. You don't kiss someone like that because you're just friends. It never went beyond kissing. It was like a silent understanding and neither of us pushed for more.

I rolled over hugging my pillow. I missed Jasper. I stared into the darkness wondering if he was still awake too.

My phone vibrated beside me.

I quickly grabbed it, mentally crossing my fingers it was Jasper. My eyes focused on the bright screen. The text was from Nick. It was an odd feeling; I was happy to hear from Nick after such a long time and yet saddened that it wasn't Jasper.

I read the message slowly.

'I'm really sorry I messed things up so badly. I hope you will forgive me. Good night my sleeping beauty. All my love. Nick'

I set my phone to the side. I was so twisted inside I didn't trust myself to respond.

In a couple of days Nick would be back at college and Jasper and I would be back at high school.

I tried to see where my path in life was going. There was a fork coming up in the road and I would have to decide which way to go.

At least I already had plans set up tomorrow with Stephanie, so I wouldn't have to decide just yet.

Chapter 19

I was at the mall by ten, waiting for Stephanie to show up. We would do a little shopping and just have a girl day.

Since it was still spring break, Daniel was home from college and he would keep little Danielle. Stephanie said he was doing well with the whole daddy thing, and she would graduate from the alternative school in May.

I sat in the food court watching people walk by. My phone went off. I read the text message from Stephanie and sighed. The baby was cranky most of the night and she was sorry, but she had to cancel.

I sat debating on what to do. The rest of my day was free and open now. Decisions would have to be made, there was no running away.

I slung my purse over my shoulder and headed toward the exit where I had parked. I was in no big hurry for what I was sure awaited me. I exited the building with the sun in my eyes. I pulled out my oversized sunglasses and put them on.

There was a group of guys to my left hanging out around the bench. I took quick notice of their behavior and was already heading out into the parking lot to avoid walking right beside them when something caught my eye.

In the middle was a tall, lanky looking kid that didn't fit in with the others. As I walked I tried to catch glimpses of what was going on without being obvious.

The group was laughing and cutting up, something had them entertained. I racked my brain for recognition of the face; I had seen him somewhere before. I was almost past the group now on the way to my car when it hit me who the person in the middle was.

I doubled back. My plan was to get a little closer and see if I was right. As I neared the group they erupted into more laughter as they made fun of the kid in the middle. As I cleared a few more feet, I knew without a doubt the one in the middle was Evan. I scanned the area looking for his parents or someone from the church. I realized there wasn't anyone else around. I was within a few feet now.

"Evan, is that you?" I called out as I approached the group.

A guy in a red t-shirt and long black saggy jean shorts turned around and eyed me. The black ink tattoo on the side of his neck read Cody.

There was something familiar about him. I mentally ran through a list of places I might know him from and came up empty. A feeling grew in the pit of my stomach, I felt like I had swallowed a brick.

He turned his attention back to the inner part of the circle. His profile sent a shock through my insides. He was the guy in the green shirt at the park the day of the attack. He was the one that Nick had pounded so mercilessly.

A sliver of fear ran through my body as I continued to approach them. I had already spoken and drew attention to myself; thoughts of going inside for help had been thwarted by that action.

I locked my eyes on Evan and continued walking toward him. "I've been looking all over for you, Evan!" I kept my voice light while silently commanding my insides to stop shaking.

Evan moved around until he could see me between the heads of two of the guys who now stood between us. "Hi!" He smiled and waved wildly. He moved forward, but the two in front of him would not allow his departure.

I stopped a few feet away. My eyes scanned the group to see if anymore from the park incident were present. A few faces I couldn't see, but the rest didn't bring any recognition.

"Come on, Evan! We've got to go, we're gonna be late." I waved for him to join me. "Everyone will look for us." I waited a few moments and added, "Tell your friends goodbye, and come on."

Evan twirled around in a circle waving, "Bye."

The same two refused to step aside. Evan, still in the circle, waited to be released.

My gut instinct told me it was now or never. I boldly stepped up and extended my arm between the two, grabbed Evan's hand and pulled him toward me. They did little more than serve as bumpers to pull Evan through.

I breathed a sigh of relief as we walked away.

"Hey, don't I know you from somewhere?"

The voice that questioned my back made my blood run cold. My heart thudded in my chest. That voice was etched into my brain, into my nightmares. A fear from deep within rose to the surface. I ignored him and kept moving toward the door, toward some form of security.

The one named Cody in the red shirt jogged up and stood in front of us. I moved to go around him when another guy sporting a crooked baseball cap, cocked down over half of his face, stood in our way.

I was trying to ignore the prickly feeling on the back of my neck that was intensifying.

Cody nodded back behind me. "You need to answer his question." His face was void of any emotion.

I stared at him through the dark-tinted glasses praying my face did not reflect the sheer fear that was enveloping me.

"No, he doesn't know me." My voice was calm. "Now move, so we can go."

"They aren't very nice." Evan complained. I squeezed his hand gently, hoping he would get the message to be quiet.

The others filtered in around us now.

I was on the edge of bolting. The only anchor that kept me from my flight was holding my hand and moving closer to me as the circle was again forming.

"I know you from somewhere." His voice was right behind me. He drew in a deep breath. "Your perfume is even familiar."

I stood silently as my knees trembled.

"So, how do I know you?" He walked past me and turned, arms crossed, his eyes trying to penetrate the dark lenses. His eyes reflected nothing.

I tried to move to the side, the surrounding ring only closed in more tightly.

"Take your glasses off." he ordered.

I shook my head. "No."

The murmurs behind me about my defiance grew louder.

At the snap of his fingers they ripped away Evan from my grasp.

"Do it, or your little friend here will wish you would have." A hint of a smile danced on his lips.

"If you're so interested, let him go inside first and then I will." The strength in my voice surprised me. The fear was being replaced by anger. Flashes of the events mixed in my head, the beating and stabbing Nick endured at his hands, the sexual assault against me.

He narrowed his eyes. "What if I say no?"

The images of that dreadful day were so real. My hand seemed to move before I knew it was moving. I slapped him hard across the cheek. He returned my slap without blinking an eye. My sunglasses skidded across the concrete walkway.

He narrowed his eyes at me. "Go ahead witch, do it again."

I obliged his request.

He caught my wrist in mid-strike. He studied me a moment. An evil smile crossed his face. "I remember you."

I focused on keeping my face from showing any kind of emotion.

Evan was whining loudly.

"Let him go inside." I clenched my teeth and jerked my wrist away from his hand.

Des stared at me through vacant eyes.

I couldn't imagine what thoughts or plans he was conjuring up. He gestured toward the door with a quick twitch of his head.

The two who held Evan prisoner escorted him in that direction.

My eyes darted to the scenery behind Des, looking for some-one who could give me some kind of help.

"Get the car!" He commanded the band of thugs around us. "We're gonna go for a little ride."

He grabbed my wrist before I could move away. His fingers biting into my flesh brought back more memories. I struggled to keep control of my emotions.

"Yeah, I do remember you now." He laughed. "Good times."

I attempted to pull my wrist away, he only tightened his grip.

He gave me an icy stare. "There will be more to come." He kissed the air. "I promise." He pulled me into the parking lot.

I tried to dig my feet in, to at least slow his progress, but my flip-flops slid along the pavement. I hit him with my free hand. Cars passed by on the outer edge of the parking lot. Watching from a distance it might appear we were playing around. I clawed at his face, drawing blood.

He stopped and turned his full attention on me. The hatred in his eyes told me there would be repercussions for my action. He drew his fist back to hammer a blow.

I turned my head, throwing my free hand out in front me and cringed, preparing for what was coming.

Something jerked me to the ground, my knee and elbow took the brunt of my weight. As soon as I felt him release my wrist, I immediately scooted away to the side.

I was aware of the throbbing and stinging in my elbow and knee, but that was the least of my worries right now. My eyes flew to where he was, expecting him to pursue.

There were two bodies rolling across the pavement. I watched closely to see who this brave soul was who had come to my rescue. They both popped to their feet. Even though his back was to me, I recognized Nick instantly.

"Wow, what a reunion." Des laughed sarcastically.

"Yeah, but it's a little more even this time." Nick countered.

They circled one another, each with his eyes glued on his adversary. The space between them was quickly closing.

Nick barely dodged Des's fist. He threw a punch striking Des in the face. His long arms gave him an advantage, he could keep a distance and still make contact.

I searched the ground for my purse. If I could get to my phone, I could call the police and hopefully end this nightmare once and for all. It was a few feet away. I kept my focus on the two who were preparing to clash again. I quietly said a prayer as I made my way in that direction.

Blood from the scrapes on my knee was running down my leg. After the park incident the whole blood thing didn't bother me as much anymore, I could stay conscious at least. I ignored the pain and hobbled toward my goal. I could hear them scuffling behind me.

The screeching of tires grabbed my attention. The group of guys had returned with the car.

I watched in horror as they piled out and headed in Nick's direction. Fear gripped my heart like a vice making me painfully aware of each beat.

"Looks like it's not so even now, rich boy. You gonna run away?" Des sneered.

I knew without him responding that Nick was not backing down. Rich's words rang in my ears, 'Your boyfriend fighting back probably saved you both.'

Unable to tear my eyes from the event about to unfold I fumbled blindly in my purse for my phone, relying on my sense of touch. My fingers wrapped around the cellular device that could be a lifeline for Nick. I quickly withdrew my hand. It got tangled in the strap of my purse and was pulled from my grasp. It clattered to the ground and slid under a nearby car. My eyes shot toward the group of guys. They were too involved in taunting Nick to notice me. I breathed a sigh of relief and worked on retrieving my phone. My knee was swelling and refused to bend without severe pain. I gently lowered myself to my good knee and stretched out my arm. I felt nothing but warm pavement. I scooted closer angling my head so that my cheek rested against the side of the car. I felt around for the phone but came up with nothing. I leaned down peering under the car. I could see it lying there. I tried again, nothing. It was just out of my reach.

The sound of feet pounding the black top pulled my attention away from my task. A blur of a person blew by the back of the car.

I rose to my feet fearing another of Des's members had now joined the throng. I scanned the group quickly trying to find the newcomer. It surprised me to see Jasper in the middle of flying fists.

He and Nick were now standing back to back thwarting any attack that might come to each other from behind. Jasper showing up caused a lull in the skirmish.

A truck ignoring the painted white parking lines headed for us at a high rate of speed.

Des was squaring off with Nick, and Cody was in Jasper's face.

Nick nodded at the truck. "It's about to get a lot more even."

A couple of the trouble makers headed to their car. The one with the crooked ball cap stood halfway between, looking uncertain if he should join the ones in the car or stick it out with the battling duo. He looked at the car and then toward the truck that was fast approaching. He quickly piled in the back seat leaving the door open behind him.

Cody was bowing out. He slowly backed toward the car. "C'mon, dude."

Des ignored his request.

Jasper moved forward, hastening Cody's retreat. He was several feet away now.

Cody jumped in the back seat and slammed the door. The engine accelerated quickly as they drove away.

The fierce look Des wore was replaced with one of unbelief as he turned to watch his boys driving away.

That split second was all Nick needed. He lunged forward knocking Des to the ground and quickly gained the upper hand.

I moved forward to watch as Nick unloaded his fury. Deep down I felt a sense of satisfaction. I was throwing punches vicariously through Nick. Des was finally getting punishment he deserved. I proceeded in their direction, my hands balled into fists at my side. I wanted to see him bleed; I wanted to see him hurt. I could feel the anger and hatred growing inside me with each step I took. The sound of flesh pounding flesh took on a whole new feeling within me now. No longer would I associate it with pain, sadness and defeat. It now meant victory, revenge, judgment, and payment being demanded in full for wrongful things done at the hands of this evil individual.

A voice grew louder in the warm morning air and it repeated one word, "Yes!"

I realized it was my voice, dripping with venom as I spurred Nick on. I stared at the face of our common enemy that was now bleeding and swollen. I could see no movement from Des; he was indeed being paid back. No smart words were coming from those lips now.

Nick's facial expression reflected the feelings I felt inside. His grunts that now accompanied each strike were like music to my ears.

A voice interrupted my thoughts. 'Is he any different from you?'

I looked around to see who spoke. No one was close by.

The question was repeated. 'Is he any different from you?'

I answered in my head. 'Yes, he's different from me.'

'Is he?'

My brain ran through the terrifying nightmares I lived out at the hands of this monster. "He's done so many terrible things." I whispered.

'Are you sinless?'

I realized the Lord was dealing with my heart. I answered silently. 'No, but I haven't done anything as bad as he has.'

'Sin is sin.'

My sense of victory faded; Des was not the true enemy here. The true enemy was not someone who could be dealt with by mere mortal human hands. This enemy could only be defeated by the blood of Jesus Christ, and it was obvious that Des did not have Jesus on his side.

A few of the guys from Nick's football team crowded around us; I recognized Big John, but the others I didn't know by name.

Jasper grabbed Nick's bloodied fist as he cocked it back ready to deliver another punishing blow. "Stop, man."

Nick jerked his arm away and glared at him. He rained down two more hits before Jasper again interfered.

"Stop!" Jasper was more forceful this time.

Nick jumped to his feet and shoved him backward. "Do you realize who this guy is?" He demanded, trying to catch his breath.

Jasper gained his balance. "Yeah, but that's enough."

Nick pushed him backward until he pinned him against the truck with a loud thud. "Do you realize what he did?" His chest was heaving. "To me?" He pointed a shaking finger in my direction. "To her?" He grabbed a wad full of Jasper's shirt in both hands. "I don't give a flip if you care what he did to me, but you better care what he did to her!" Spit flew from his mouth as he snarled out his words through clenched teeth.

Jasper remained calm. "I do care, but killing him will not change any of it."

Nick released his grip. "No, but it'll make me feel better." He turned and walked back to Des, a fire burning in his eyes.

Jasper clamped his arms around Nick from behind. "No!"

That was all he could get out before Nick grabbed him.

It happened so fast it was just a blur. Somehow Nick flipped Jasper around and they were both wrestling on the pavement.

I was ushered along with the guys from the team heading toward the two friends who were returning blow for blow.

The sound of a car door drew everyone's attention. They had returned for Des and quickly loaded him into the back seat. Two of the football guys sprinted after the car, giving up the chase after a few yards.

Two Police cruisers raced across the parking lot heading for our group.

They separated Nick and Jasper to keep the peace.

It didn't take long for the four officers to sort everyone into groups and take statements.

Jasper and Nick were each escorted to the back of separate squad cars.

I answered questions as I watched them being patted down. I pointed in their direction. "They aren't criminals."

The officer ignored my comments and continued his line of questioning. He didn't even give me the courtesy of looking up from his notepad.

"You're not hearing me. They are NOT criminals! Why are you treating them that way?" My statement that started out so strong was quickly crumbling. "They were protecting me."

"Weren't they the ones fighting when we arrived?" His voice was cold and uncaring. He stood a little taller than me, his mirrored sunglasses reflected my image back at me.

My bottom lip bounced with emotion. I didn't need to make things worse for them. Looking at it from his perspective I would probably assume the same thing. He couldn't begin to understand without knowing the full story and I didn't want to spell it out for yet another stranger. I stared at the nametag on his uniform.

Officer Smith's features softened slightly. "Do you need medical attention?" He squatted down to look at my swollen, bruised knee. The bleeding had stopped, leaving a trail of brownish red streaks down my shin.

"I just want to go home." I whispered.

He helped me over to his cruiser where I sat on the edge of the back seat with the door open. Nick was standing at the rear of the car with his back to me. I could see frustration in his gestures as he tried to explain his side of the story.

I had a growing feeling that the past would keep popping up in my face when I least expected it. How could I put something behind me that refused to go away?

The temperature felt like it had increased tremendously. I wiped sweat from my forehead with the back of my hand and wondered how much longer before we could leave.

"Oh, come on!" Nick raised his voice. "You're kidding me!"

The officer had him up against the back of the car cuffing his hands behind his back.

Nick was furious.

I quickly looked over to where Jasper stood. He was talking casually to the officer, no sign of distress. He didn't seem to be aware of the situation on this side.

The Officer with short, spiked, blonde hair spoke with the one standing beside Nick. A few moments later he walked over and spoke with Jasper.

The taller Police Officer who was talking to the football players closed his notepad and walked in our direction. Big John and the others loaded up in the truck and drove away.

I walked to the back of the car defying the stiffness in my knee. I read the name tag on the uniform before making eye contact as I approached.

"Can I talk to him?"

Officer Moore nodded his head.

Nick's jaw was clenched as he stared straight ahead. His chest rose and fell in a huff, anger apparent on his face.

"Are you ok?" I asked softly.

He raised his arms slightly showing off his cuffs, "Yeah, I'm great." He snorted. He looked down at me out of the corner of his eye, keeping his face forward. His eyes dropped to my knee and then back to my face. "You ok?"

I stood in front of him peering up. His lip was swollen and bleeding, and his right cheek was bruised. This was becoming commonplace for him. I stared at his chest blinking back tears as reality was slowly catching up.

He spoke again, his voice not as stern. "I'm ok, Em." He stepped forward and rested his cheek on the top of my head. "It's okay now."

I slid my arms around his waist. The sound of his heartbeat brought comfort. I shook my head. "I don't think it will ever end."

The blonde officer returned. "Un-cuff him."

I moved as Officer Moore produced a key and worked on the

cuffs.

"Pastor Owens isn't pressing charges."

My head snapped in Jasper's direction. "Why is Pastor Wayne here?" I looked at Nick, confused.

He rubbed his wrist where the cuffs had been. "Because he's Jasper's Dad."

My thoughts immediately went back to that night in Pastor's office when he told me he was being unbiased. I assumed he meant because Nick and Jasper both attended his church. I tried to hide my surprise.

Nick watched me closely. "Didn't know he was a PK, huh?"

I ran through ideas of what PK could mean without making a connection. "A what?"

"A preacher's kid."

I thought preacher's kids were all pristine. Jasper didn't strike me as a PK, not that he was a bad person, and not that I had any knowledge of what a PK was really like, anyway. I quickly pushed my thoughts aside as Jasper walked up.

The officers in the cruiser opposite of us was already driving off.

"I'm not pressing charges." Jasper stopped a few feet away from Nick and stuck his hands halfway in the front of his jeans pockets.

I studied his face taking in the damage. His nose had been bloodied, he had a fat lip, and his eye would be black before tomorrow. I wandered which of those Nick inflicted and which resulted from the struggle with Des's crew.

Nick's jaw was clenched again. He crossed his arms and stared hard at Jasper. "It doesn't change anything." He stated firmly.

Jasper shrugged. "Whatever you need to do, man."

Officer Moore remained close by watching the exchange, ready to step in if needed.

I could feel the tension between these two, who at one point recently, were good friends. I felt awkward knowing I was the reason they were at odds.

"Are you okay, Emma?" Jasper stooped and examined my knee.

"I'm ok." Remembering the last time he had examined an injury I had, I gently moved his hand away.

He straightened and pulled me into a hug. "I'm sorry if I hurt you just now."

I returned his gesture of compassion. "You didn't."

Officer Moore cleared his throat. "You all need to head home, or wherever it is your going."

Jasper dropped his arms. "I'll drive you home."

"I'll drive her home!" Nick interjected.

"I think you need to go somewhere and cool off before you get into trouble." Officer Moore's voice was stern as he spoke to Nick.

Nick gave Jasper one more long stare. "I'll be by later to check on you, Em, after he's gone." He turned and walked away without another word. I watched him cross the parking lot, head held high and shoulders back.

Jasper took me home and got my knee cleaned up. My elbow was sore, and that was the extent of the damage.

Mom worried that Des was still out on the streets somewhere.

I quickly became a prisoner in my own life. I could no longer go anywhere by myself. I couldn't be at home alone, and if I was out, I had to call and check in every hour. In public places I caught myself scanning every person in a room or group before entering. As much as I wanted to move on, I just couldn't.

Jasper was usually with me and assured me he would protect me. I had cooled the jets on any relationship that was there before. Part of my heart still yearned for Nick, and it was in limbo. I was content having both in my life. I had Jasper during the week and Nick on the weekends.

Week after week went by with no more sightings of Des, but I couldn't put my fears to rest. There were times the hairs on the back of my neck let me know he was close by, even if I couldn't see him, I knew he was there. He was waiting and watching for his time to strike back.

About the Author

I hope you really enjoyed the book. Here are a few things about me:

I live with my husband and our family in the Ozarks in the United States. I love cooking with my husband, and spending time with my family, laughing and having fun. There is never a dull moment!

I enjoy going to the beach, but also love the snow. My passion is writing stories to share with others.

Other books I have written:

Inevitable - Changes Trilogy Book 1

You can follow me on my Facebook page: Robin Worden Inevitable Book Page and you can check out my web page: RobinWorden.com

Acknowledgements

There are several people I would like to thank; the first one is my Savior, Jesus. He gave me a creative mind and the desire to write. I have so much to be thankful for.

Thank you to my immediate family: Bob, Kristina & Greg, Jessica & Justin, Taylor, and Alyssa. You have put up with me being on the computer, laptop, phone, and tablet for hours on end again, for this second book. You guys are amazing, and I appreciate your support more than you know.

Thank you to my family and many friends for believing in me. I appreciate those who took time to read over the book and let me know what you thought: Bob W, Kristina P, Jessica M. P, Kevin H, Billie H, Christy O, Kristy T, Beth M, Charlena H, Jessica P, Emma S, and Melinda T. You are all awesome!

One Last Thing

If you have enjoyed reading this book, I'd be very grateful if you would please tell your friends about my book and post a review on Amazon. Your support makes a difference; thank you.

Dedication

I dedicate this book to my family and friends. I love all of you!